Frances Brooke

**The History of Charles Mandeville**

A Sequel to Lady Julia

Frances Brooke

**The History of Charles Mandeville**
*A Sequel to Lady Julia*

ISBN/EAN: 9783743441668

Manufactured in Europe, USA, Canada, Australia, Japa

Cover: Foto ©Andreas Hilbeck / pixelio.de

Manufactured and distributed by brebook publishing software (www.brebook.com)

Frances Brooke

**The History of Charles Mandeville**

# THE

# HISTORY

## OF.

# CHARLES MANDEVILLE.

A

SEQUEL TO LADY JULIA,

By Mrs. BROOKE.

DUBLIN:

PRINTED FOR CHAMBERLAINE AND RICE, P. WOGAN,
P. BYRNE, H. COLBERT, W. M'KENZIE, J. MOORE,
J. JONES, GRUEBER, AND M'ALLISTER,
W. JONES, G. DRAPER, R. WHITE,

M,DCC,XC,

# INTRODUCTION.

To Mrs. S.———

WHEN I agreed to comply with my dear friend's requeſt, of collecting an account of the incidents that have happened in the Mandeville Family, ſince thoſe unfortunate events, which you, (and all who have hearts,) have grieved for, I had the greateſt proſpect of accompliſhing the taſk better, than I now find I am able to do.

My

My intimacy with Lady Anne Belville, made me truft to every affiftance her lively wit could give me; and as fhe was fo conftantly at Belmont, before fhe married Colonel Belville, her information muft be authentic; but her wit and fpirit is turned into another channel! that flow of humour, which ufed to divert all who heard it, is now wholly employed in enlivening domeftic fcenes! It adorns the moft improved underftanding, and makes her fhine as an amiable wife, and tender mother.

She frankly told me, that Lady Julia Mandeville's death had fo damped her fpirit for writing letters, that were fhe now to take up the pen, her ftyle would be

funk

funk into that of a mere ftory-teller; that perhaps if fhe fpoke truth, fhe muft own fhe fhould feel herfelf mortified at this change, as fhe was once vain of her epifto-lary talents; yet, fhe muft confefs, fhe thought her time and talents were now better employed; but though fhe could not affift me with her pen, fhe would gra-tify me, by giving me all the papers fhe could collect, that I might digeft them into fuch order, as would enable me to carry on the thread of the ftory; and fhe would hereafter inform me of thofe facts that were not to be found in thofe manufcripts.

You fee, therefore, my dear madam, I am going to fea, without the fkilful pilot I had depended upon! you muft therefore

fore excuſe the errors, that will unavoid-
ably be the conſequence.　But I flatter myſelf, the deſire to obey any command of
your's, will, in ſome meaſure, compen-
ſate for the defects of,

My dear Mrs. S.——

Your very affectionate Friend,

JANE P.——

# THE

# HISTORY

## OF

## CHARLES MANDEVILLE.

To Mifs KITTY FORTESCUE.

My deareft friend,

A H! with what anguifh do I give that title to any body, but my beloved Julia! yet I can truly fay, I love you fincerely; and its giving a relief to my forrows, to write to you, is a fure proof that I do.—Sorrows, which I would not part with, though I am pleafed to have them foftened by the tender and fenfible remarks in your kind and fympathizing letter. I do, believe me, I do try, to the utmoft of my power, to exert every

B                                        faculty,

faculty, and employ all the arguments, my own reafon, and your better fenfe points out, to enable me to bear my fad fate as a Chriftian ought! but nature will—nay, it muft feel; and my heart is too little to contain fo much grief, without fometimes overflowing. Never, till now, did I know the pangs of affliction! I was too young when my parents died, to be fenfible of their lofs; and have been bleffed with fuch friends, that I have never known the want of parental tendernefs. Moft comfortable, indeed, is your reply to my long tale of woe. You allow me to indulge my fond wifhes, in the hope of meeting my dear Julia in a ftate of perfect blifs!—this gives forrow a pillow to reft upon!

We are all in better health, than, confidering our miferable fituation, could have been expected. God is ever merciful! That fure truft and confidence we repofe in him, has enabled us to endeavour to fweeten the bitter cup, each has drank fo largely of. The heart-ftricken parents, feem, indeed, like monuments of woe; yet,

with

with amazement, Lady'Anne Wilmot and myfelf, obferve the fubmiffive fortitude they fhew,
till fome accidental occurrence revives emotions
too ftrong to be fuppreffed—then, with eyes
moiftened with forrow, they haftily retire; as
poor Lord Belmont was forced to do, but an
hour ago. I hear Lady Anne's ftep ; fhe is com-
ing with her wonted goodnefs to foothe me ; or,
perhaps, to fteal away one difmal hour, to relieve our minds by converfation——were it not
for her, I think I muft have fank into my Julia's
grave, before this time.

I was miftaken, Lady Anne came to tell me,
fhe met my Lord alone, in too penfive a mood ;
and has perfuaded him, it would be of great ufe
to my health, if he could prevail upon me to take
a ride this fine afternoon. The fweet, amiable
man, (not fufpecting the defign to amufe him)
faid, if I would ride, he would accompany me;
provided, Lady Anne would be fo kind as to
amufe Lady Belmont in our abfence. You may
be fure I do not hefitate—-it is my mind's beft

cor-

cordial, to pleafe thofe whom my Julia loved.—
Oh! that for their fakes, as well as my own, I
could change places with her.—Yet, does not
this found prophane and felfifh ? as if murmur-
ing at the decrees of Providence, and envying
her the joys of heaven! Indeed, I do not mean
either; but my thoughts were ever wont to out-
run my reafon; ah! what wonder they fhould
do fo now?—fhe, who ufed to correct thofe
thoughts, is gone! and that reafon is clouded
with forrow. Alas! error muft be the confequence, when I am left without my kind and
prudent monitor. But I muft now quit my pen,
and prepare to attend his Lordfhip.

## IN CONTINUATION.

Alas! my dear Kitty, when we rife in the
morning, how little do we forefee the anxiety
we may have to contend with ere night. Affliction has taught me to moralize; whilft it has
added to my natural inability to write well;
therefore, without any farther preface, than
adoring

adoring that divine power, which has this day fhewn fuch mercy to us all, I will relate a ' plain, ' unvarnifhed tale,' which wants no rhetorical ornaments to engage your attention.

You remember, I laid down my pen to attend my Lord. We took horfe at the little gate of the park—I trembled on obferving his Lordfhip turn up his eyes to Lady Julia's chamber window : he fighed heavily, and wiped away the tears, which ran down his venerable cheeks ; anfwering the fervant's queftion of ' which way ' his Lordfhip chofe to ride,' by faying, ' afk ' Mifs Howard, all places are now alike to me.' I faid the moft fhady was preferable, as the fun was very hot. Worthy George had his leffon from Lady Anne ; whofe good head, and better heart, had pointed out the route, leaft likely to meet any body ; and not accuftomed to be taken formerly, though a pleafant one.

We followed George through fhady lanes, full of melodious chorifters ; whofe harmony muft have

have enlivened any heart, not entirely benumb-
ed with forrow. Indeed it appeared to have
fome effect on my Lord ; for he ftopped to
liften, and then repeated fix lines out of the
Shunamite—' Righteous, and good, art Thou,
' &c.' We ftopped again where the river was
running in meanders, on the fide of a lovely
meadow, to obferve an old houfe which feemed
newly, and elegantly repaired. My Lord afked
George, who it was now inhabited that ancient
manfion ? George replied, ' a Mr. Ware, who
' had acquired a large fortune in trade, had
' bought the eftate ; that he was a very worthy
' gentleman, and already beloved by the whole
' village ; to whom he was a blefﬁng." " Why,
' furely,' faid my Lord, ' this cannot be Mea-
' dow-Houfe, we cannot have rode fo far ; it is
' above fix miles from Belmont.' On the fervant's replying in the affirmative ; my Lord faid,
' then we will only go to that corner, to take a
' view of the river, and return home.'

As we rode flowly on, we faw a gentleman at
a diftance, which made my Lord turn his horfe
quick

quick about; when a shot rook, nearly dead, fluttered up a little way off the ground, and startled the horse : his Lordship, being off his guard, was thrown into the river, in the most rapid part of the stream.

Imagine my terrors, for no words can describe them : yet I had senses enough left to call loudly to George, who immediately jumped off his horse, and was going to leap into the river, when the gentleman we had observed before, flew, like a bird, to the water side; and throwing off his clothes, gave his watch to the servant, saying, ' take care of the lady, I can swim fast, and hope ' to save the gentleman ;" so plunged into the river, and in a little time, (though to me it seemed a very long one) he caught my Lord, just as he reached the mill ; and at length brought him, oh ! joyful sight, on the meadow ; and, after holding him up, that he might discharge the water he had swallowed, he bore him in his arms towards the house. As he passed George, he bid him tell the lady the gentleman would soon be well, and desired she would fol-

low

low them. George, I believe, faved me from fainting, by his news: for as I was running towards the river, I faw blood on the grafs, and concluded my Lord was killed. George told me, the blood came from the gentleman's arm ; which was torn by the mill, juft as he ftretched it, to take hold of him ; but for all that, he did not let him go. My grateful heart fupplicated heaven, for bleffings on my Lord's preferver.

When I firft faw him in his walk, I had remarked a peculiar dignity, and noble, manly port ; but now I fuppofed him fome celeftial being, fent to fave my Lord.

I walked to the houfe, as faft as my trembling limbs would carry me, revolving, in my mind, what melancholy confequences might follow from this accident, though the immediate danger was over.

A decent female fervant met me with drops and water, and begged I would lean upon her ;

for

for she saw I could hardly support myself, and was unable to speak. She told me, the gentleman was put into bed, and so much recovered, as to desire to see the lady. This account gave a pleasing relief to my spirits, and enabled me to quicken my pace.

I found my Lord sitting up in bed, and just going to drink a glass of cyprus wine.—' Emily,' said he, ' that gentleman has saved my life, at the ' hazard of his own—tell this to Lady Belmont, ' and Colonel Mandeville—" He was proceeding, when the gentleman returned; having been absent to change his clothes.

He begged my Lord would not talk much at present; then bowing to me, begged my pardon; but he believed, from the sweet disposition my countenance expressed, he should think, the best respect he could pay me, was to take care of my father; therefore he would make no apology for any want of proper attendance, as he had dispatched his servants for a physician, and a sur-

geon,

geon, left my patient should suffer from ignorance.   He then felt my Lord's pulse, and cast-
ing on me the finest pair of blue eyes I ever beheld, said, with a smile, as if it were an earnest
of pleasing news, ' the pulse are now nearly as re-
' gular as if nothing had happened; let me in-
' treat you, madam, to drink this glass of wine;
' it will help you to recover your fright." I
obeyed, and felt its glowing warmth revive me;
but soon sunk again, by seeing drops of blood on
the sheets; my Lord observed them at the same
moment, and perceiving they came from the gentleman's gown sleeve, hastily called out, Oh!
' sir, I fear you are greatly hurt.' ' Only enough
' to excuse my appearing in so improper a garb,
' as this loose night-gown; but I will retire,
' and soon stop the blood, if you will promise
' me to repose here to-night; as rest for a few
' hours, and then some proper nourishment,
' will be necessary before you remove." This
was assented to, by my Lord, who repeated his
request to Mr. Ware, to be careful of himself.
Mr. Ware then asked where he should send, to

prevent

prevent his family's being uneafy at his abfence? My Lord, faid, I fhould write a few lines, and difpatch his fervant with them.

Mr. Ware went away, fending in writing materials dire&ly: and I wrote a fhort billet to my Lady; to which my Lord added a line or two. He then afked me, if I did not perceive a ftrong refemblance in Mr. Ware's voice, to that of our poor loft Harry. I confeffed, it had ftruck me; but added, there was no refemblance in the face. His Lordfhip, weakened by his late accident, could not command himfelf, fo well as he ufually does, but burft into a flood of tears. As I dreaded the effe&s of any great emotion at this time, I changed the fubje&, and requefted him to lie down, and try to compofe himfelf to reft. He did fo, and fooner than I could have expe&ed, fell into a found fleep.

I ftole out of the room, to take my letter to George, and found Mr. Ware in the adjoining
apartment,

apartment, who affured me, he would take my
place, and watch the gentleman, calling the
houfe-keeper to conduct me into the parlour, and
order my fervant to attend me.

Poor George was tranfported he had fuch good
news to carry; but, ' Ah! madam,' faid he,
' the poor gentleman's arm is fadly hurt, indeed;
' the flefh is torn up to the fhoulder; and in
' one place, fo much fo, as to fhew the bone.
' The coachman and I have bound it up, by his
' orders, with fome herbs, which he fetched out
' of his clofet: the doing it, made me fhudder,
' yet he hardly winched.'

I haftened George away, and was alone for
two hours; as the coming of the phyfician and
furgeon, made me think it improper to go up
ftairs.   Mercy on me, how did I wifh for judgment to act right?—how did I want Lady Anne's
difcretion to direct my conduct?  As I was pon-
dering what I ought to do, the houfe-keeper came

to inform me, the gentleman was awake, and wanted to fpeak to me.

I flew up ftairs—his Lordfhip faid, ' My dear ' Emily, I wifh you would go to Belmont, to ' affure Lady Belmont I am perfectly well, and ' would go home to-night, but for my promife ' to Mr. Ware, that I would ftay till morning. ' The phyfician and furgeon have been here, ' and both affure me I have received no injury. ' Indeed, I feel quite well; but I fear my pre- ' ferver is very bad, and very obftinate; he will ' not permit the furgeon to apply any other ' dreffing to his arm than fome herbs, he brought ' from abroad. He is gone to bed; and I can ' fee, plainly, the phyfician thinks ill of him. ' I hope he will mend to-morrow, and that I ' fhall be fo happy as to leave him better; for ' I fhall be miferable, if his kindnefs to me ' fhould prove deftructive to himfelf." At this moment, I was called out, and found Lady Anne was come for me.

Heaven

Heaven preferve my dear Kitty from ever experiencing fuch affecting trials, as has lately been the lot of her

EMILY HOWARD.

To

## To Miss KITTY FORTESCUE.

I Suppose Emily has long since introduced me to your acquaintance, by giving you my history; as young friends make it the criterion of amity, to tell all they know, which they term, increasing joy, and lessening sorrow, by decanting (if you will allow the phrase, it was the first that occurred, and I never study) every thought into each others breast, till they overflow with tears of sympathy. I will, therefore, not look upon myself as a stranger; but lay aside my own flippant pen, and take up the more sober one of your friend, and try to catch her plain unaffected manner, that you may read her words in my hand-writing, as I have insisted on her going to bed, to try to compose her too much agitated spirits.

When

When I arrived at Meadow Houfe, I found the dear girl in a fluctuating ftate of mind; doubting the propriety of her remaining there alone, yet unwilling to leave my Lord, though he had requefted her to return.—My arrival, removed thefe difficulties.

We had been made uneafy at Belmont, by their long abfence—minds, that have been fet to melancholy tones, ever play the moft difmal tunes—all, privately thought fome misfortune had happened; yet each faid the beft they could devife, to prove they did not : but as the time paffed on, we grew more impatient, and fervants were fent out different ways  One met George ; the found of horfes, brought the alarmed trio to the door.  George wifely faid, " My Lord, and " Mifs Howard, are both well, but do not re- " turn to-night, fo fent me with this letter."

Lady Belmont, with a countenance as pale as a ghoft, took the paper with trembling hands ; and

and finding herself unable to open it, I read aloud Emily's account, which was as follows.

'  ' My dear Lady,

' An angel of a man has faved my Lord from
' receiving any injury by his horfe's throwing him
' into the river; but, as he was thoroughly
' wet, you may fuppofe, Mr. Ware took him to
' his houfe, and ordered a bed to be warmed, and
' has prevailed on his Lordfhip to lie down,
' whilft his clothes were dried.  I am affured,
' and, indeed, fee every reafon to believe, he
' has not met with the leaft hurt by the accident,
' formidable as it appeared ; but for fear of taking
' cold, Mr. Ware has prevailed on him to fleep
' here to-night.  I will not detain the fervant,
' to add an unneceffary line from

'  ' Your dutiful, and obliged

'  ' EMILY HOWARD.''

Then followed, in my Lord's hand-writing, thefe few lines.

' My

' My deareſt love,

' Emily ſays true, for I am perfectly well,
' thanks to Heaven ; and Mr. Ware, who has,
' at the hazard of his own life, ſaved that of

' Your ever devoted

' BELMONT."

Joy, terror, and grief, ſo occupied poor Lady
Belmont's mind, that they denied her the power
of ſpeech ; but ſhe looked ſo piteouſly at me, that
I plainly read her wiſhes, and obeyed them, by
ordering the poſt chaiſe to be immediately got
ready ; ſaying, My Lord's gentleman, and myſelf, would go to him with freſh clothes.

Whilſt theſe matters were preparing, I prevailed on her Ladyſhip to go to bed, as the anxiety of her mind for ſome hours, and the agitation
this account gave her, made me fear for her
health.

We

We arrived at Meadow Houſe as ſoon as it was poſſible. My Lord was ſo well, and ſo much re-freſhed by his ſleep, that he had got up, and was dreſſed in a morning gown of Mr. Ware's. He told me that poor gentleman was the only ſuffe-rer by this accident; and that his being ſo hurt, on his account, had made him leſs reluctant to ſtay, that he might ſee him in the morning; and then he, would return to his dear wife.—He wiſhed me to go back directly to her, and take Emily with me.

We got home by eleven. After ſeeing Emily in bed, as ſhe wanted ſleep, I was going to reſt; but not yet—fate had decreed my thoughts full employment; for before I reached my dreſſing-room, I heard a ſoft, but heavy foot, and my name gently called.——It proved the dejected Colonel Mandeville. Conceiving he wanted ſome intelligence, I was glad of it, for curioſity is a great help to diſpel grief. I ſtopped, and he begged my pardon for the interruption, and per-miſſion for a few minutes converſation.

The

The moment we entered my dreffing-room, he threw himfelf on a fopha, and burft into a flood of tears. I was amazed, as I had never feen him weep in all our forrows, and began to difperfe his fears for my Lord, when he haftily faid, ' Oh! Lady Anne, affift my diftracted ' mind to unfold this myftery! the watch! oh! ' the watch!'——I ftarted, and really began to fear his brain was difturbed.

In a few minutes, he compofed himfelf fufficiently to fay, ' Soon after you went, George came ' into the parlour, afking leave to go directly ' back to Meadow Houfe, for that Mr. Ware, ' juft as he leaped into the river, gave him the ' watch he then held in his hand; and with a ' remarkable earneft look, bid him take care of ' it, and give it him fafe again; but, faid ' George, the fright I was in for my Lord, and ' the helping to affift poor Mr. Ware afterwards, ' put it out of my head; pray let me carry it directly; for can I do too much for one that has ' faved my Lord?

' It

‘ It is too late, faid I ; I will take care of it to-
‘ night, and you fhall go with it early in the
‘ morning.

‘ George retired, leaving the watch on the
‘ table ; I foon after took it up to look at the
‘ hour ; the feal catched in my ruffle ; and as I
‘ was difengaging it, the arms caught my eye.—
‘ Oh ! my good God, what fhall I think ? it
‘ is the very feal I gave my poor boy Charles,
‘ with our arms and creft ; nay, it is, I verily
‘ believe, the fame watch I gave him ; but the
‘ feal I am pofitive is the fame.

‘ He was loft in the Victory ! my partial fond-
‘ nefs for my ever to be lamented Harry, made
‘ me too foon forget my Charles ! Righteous Hea-
‘ ven ! I have been juftly punifhed for my
‘ faults !’——

Here he ftopped ; forrow left him only the
power of fighs to exprefs his feelings !

I was

I was much aftonifhed—after a moment's reflection, told him, Mr. Ware could doubtlefs
give fome light into this ftrange affair ; but that
I feared he was very ill, with the hurt he had received ; and then I related all that had paffed at
Meadow Houfe, and what I had heard from
Emily.

The Colonel rofe, lifted his hands and eyes to·
heaven, and withdrew in filence.

I went to bed, but not to reft ; however I was
refrefhed, and rofe early, and went to Emily ;
who I found had not been able to fleep, and had
a violent head ach ; faid fhe was going to rife, for
fhe muft finifh a letter to you, time enough for
the poft. I told her I would do that, if fhe would
try to fleep an hour or two.

'Will you be fo good,. my dear Lady Anne ?
'my letter lies on the table, read it, for I have
'no fecrets I want to hide from you, and add
'what you think proper.'

I looked

I looked over her lines, and when I came to
' the dignity of air and manner, and fine blue
' eyes,' I caſt my eyes archly on her's. She
bluſhed, and looked down. This, with ſome
few things ſhe had ſaid about this ſame ſtranger,
as we returned home, made me ſuſpect the fire
of thoſe ſame fine blue eyes had kindled a ſpark
in her tender heart, and might raiſe an unuſual
flame, in a breaſt that had hitherto felt only the
more gentle warmth of friendſhip; but to confeſs the truth, I do not wiſh for more love ſcenes
at Belmont, leſt they ſhould only be tragic ones,
ſo changed the ſubject; and when I had prated
to her a few minutes, went into the parlour,
where I found the anxious Colonel folding a
letter; he read me the contents, which, as nearly as I can recollect, were as follow——

' Pardon, ſir, the diſtreſſing anxiety of an
' unhappy old man; I mean not to be imperti-
' nent, but the ſeal to your watch, has awakened
' every feeling: it bears my coat of arms, and
' creſt; and was once given by me to my ſon
'                                        ' Charles

' Charles Mandeville, who was loſt in the Vic-
' tory man of war.   Perhaps he gave that token
' of juvenile (conſequently  pure)  affection to
' you.  Gladly would I wait on the man my dear
' boy loved, even if I had not reaſon to bleſs you,
' for having been the preſerver of my greatly ho-
' nored friend; therefore, as ſoon as  your phy-
' ſician thinks company not improper for you,  I
' mean  to pay my reſpects to you,  and am, ſir,
' with the moſt ardent wiſhes for your recovery,

   ' Your's, &c.

    ' CHARLES MANDEVILLE.'


 George immediately ſet out with the watch and
letter ; the coach had before gone for my Lord ;
Lady Belmont was retired to  her room ; and I
began to have a little leiſure to indulge my own
thoughts.  My imagination, like a ventilator in
a window, is for ever going round ; and it often
brings back the horrors paſt, and as often pre-
ſents me with pleaſing hope for the future, by
thinking with joy on my own dear Colonel.

       Colonel

Colonel Mandeville faid he would walk (I could guefs where) to feed his forrows, when a meffenger arrived from London with a letter, defiring him inftantly to fet off to fee a dying friend, and intreating him not to delay a moment. He requefted I would fend the letter directly to him, but hoped to be again at Belmont, in four or five days at fartheft.

Emily's maid informs me her miftrefs is awake, and much better. The poft-man ftays, fo I will clofe this hiftory, rather than letter, by affuring you,

I am, madam,

Your, &c.

ANNE WILMOTT.

C

To

To Colonel BELLVILLE.

I DO not remonftrate, and diffemble as I
fhould have done a few months paft, when my
fpirits were more blithe ; but either won by your
merit, or betrayed by my own heart, I give up
the point, and fairly own, I cannot contradict
the force of your arguments ; fo confefs, I wifh
to fee you here, and to accompany you to Lady
Mary, in order to expedite my niece, Bell Haftings' happinefs ; that when the neceffary appearance in a court of juftice is over, nothing may
remain to delay the match ; for fince the late
deplorable fcenes here, I muft ever fear for lovers, till their hands, as well as hearts, are
united.

A little

A little funſhine ſeems to gleam upon Belmont : may gracious Heaven grant it may diſſipate the black cloud which has ſo long enveloped us !

I am willing to give you hopes of meeting us leſs diſmal.—My Lord's ſafe return (after the tremendous accident my laſt informed you of) gave Lady Belmont more tranſport than I ever expe&ted to ſee her feel.

'Emily flew down ſtairs to welcome him, and then with her ſerious, innocent, and artleſs look, eagerly aſked—' How is Mr. Ware ?' He an-ſwered, very gravely—' Very ill, I fear !' Down went Emily's eyes, whilſt her ears liſtened eagerly to my Lord, who went on, ſaying, ' He ' adds to my apprehenſions for him, by his ob- ' ſtinacy, for he will not permit his arm to be ' dreſſed with any thing but thoſe herbs ; and ' told me this morning, he had known that ap- ' plication effe&t greater cures than this would ' be, in two days, yet he cannot ſtir his arm at ' all. He aſked for you, Emily, and is very

C 2                              ' uneaſy

' uneafy about a watch, which he fays he values
' above all other treafures; I concluded there-
' fore he was delirious, fo left his bed-fide.


' He is immoderately fond of a wonderfully
' pretty little girl.' (Emily coloured; ha! ha!
thought I, fo he is married.) ' The child is very
' young, and though it prates faft, can hardly
' be underftood: it is fo beautiful, I thought on
' what once was——'


My Lord fighed, and paufed, but foon recovered from his agitation; then proceeding faid,
' My benefactor is a foreigner, I believe; for
' though he fpeaks Englifh better than moft peo-
' ple do, who have not learned it young; yet
' he fpeaks it flowly, and with hefitation. I
' find he has not been long in England; howe-
' ver, let him be of what country he may, his
' manners are agreeable; his converfation difco-
' vers fenfe and good-nature; and there is a
' remarkable grandeur in his deportment, that
' proves him to be a man of confequence.

' Juft

' Juſt as I left his room, having ordered my
' coach to the door, I perceived a neat equipage,
' that would not let my carriage drive up.   A
' gentleman got out, and having enquired of
' my ſervants who they belonged to, approach-
' ed me with great reſpect, ſaying, I was very
' kind indeed, thus to honor his friend, in his
' ſolitary ſtate.   He ſeemed much ſhocked at
' hearing he was ill; ſaid he was the mildeſt,
' braveſt, and honeſteſt man he had ever known.

' After a little diſcourſe, I found I was talking
' then to Mr. Ware, the owner of the ſeat; and
' that my preſerver's name was Woodville.

' Mr. Ware ſaid,  he had brought him very
' good news;  for that two ſhips, laden with
' immenſe treaſures, were ſafe in the Downs.
' Mr. Ware begged  I would permit him, after
' he had ſeen his friend, to accompany me home;
' but I aſſured him, he would confer a  much
' greater obligation on me, by ſtaying to take
' care of Mr. Woodville.

' To-

' To-morrow I intend to pay a vifit to Mr.
' Ware, and the poor fufferer; and I wifh, la-
' dies, you would accompany me, to wait on
' Mrs. Ware, and her fifter, who came down
' this morning with Mr. Ware ; as our beft civi-
' lities are furely due to every inhabitant of that
' houfe.'

We all affented.   Now if this fame foreigner,
with his two fhips full of riches,  proves a bache-
lor——no, that cannot be, for here is a little
girl.  Well, perhaps he may be a widower——
aye, that is the cafe, to be fure ; it accounts
fo well for his mourning.   Why then, I think
there will be one more bride at Belmont, than
your foolifh

ANNE WILMOTT.

To

## To Colonel BELLVILLE.

OH dear! oh dear! I am out of breath with events; they crowd so fast upon me, I know not where to begin. I wish you were here to regulate my confused ideas; but on reflection, I think its possible you might encrease their confusion; so, perhaps, it is better as it is.

Well, I will try for a little method, and proceed to tell you, that for a few hours we were in quietness, when we began to wonder that George was not returned. After dinner, he arrived with a letter to Colonel Mandeville. My Lord enquired why he had delayed so long. Take his own story——

‘ I was

' I was fhewn up to the gentleman's room ;
' he told me his arm was much eafier, and was
' fure it would foon be quite well ; he took the
' watch, and very obligingly thanked me for the
' care of it ; he looked earneftly at it ; fighed,
' and preffed it to his heart. He then opened
' the letter ; and cafting his eyes on the name,
' his colour went and came ; and he ordered lit-
' tle mifs, who was fitting in his lap, to go to
' her maid, which the pretty creature did im-
' mediately ; he then read the letter, and fell
' into fuch an agony, I thought he was dying :
' being alone with him, I was fadly frightened,
' and ventured to ring the bell violently ; pre-
' fently in ran the gentleman, who it feems ar-
' rived juft as your Lordfhip went away ; two
' fervants followed, fo I thought it proper for
' me to leave the chamber.

' The two fervants foon came down ; and told
' me, I was to wait for an anfwer to the letter I
' had brought. I thought it long before it came ;
' but they faid, Mr. Woodville (who, it feems
' is

' is the fick gentleman, and he that came to-
' day is Mr. Ware) was in a ftrange diforder;
' the fervants whifpered, that by the ftrange
' things he faid, they believed he was out of
' his fenfes.

' At laft, Mr. Ware came down, and brought
' me this letter; faying, the one I had brought,
' had difordered his friend fo much, that his arm
' began to bleed afrefh, and the furgeon found
' him much worfe; but they hoped the fame re-
' medy that had ferved him before, would be
' again effectual; but that he had found much
' difficulty in writing the few lines I was to carry
' home.'

George being gone down, my Lord looked at
the letter very earneftly—the feal caught his eyes,
and excited more furprize. I thought it moft
prudent to conceal what Colonel Mandeville had
faid about that feal. My Lord declared he never
before had felt an inclination to do fo difhonou-
rable a thing as breaking the feal of another per-

fon's

fon's letter; he then laid it down. I took it, and retiring, wrote a few lines to inform Colonel Mandeville of his Lordſhip's being returned well; and incloſing this ſame letter, diſpatched it by my own ſervant to town.

I was called to prayers, at which all the ſervants attended; and my Lord returned public thanks for his late great eſcape.

I find myſelf ſo fatigued with the various perturbations I have gone through, that I can only add, that I am more your's than my own,

ANNE WILMOTT.

To

To Miſs KITTY FORTESCUE.

[After repeating moſt of what has been found in Lady
   Anne's letter, ſhe goes on to ſay,]

WE all retired to gain ſome needful reſt ; but
ſhall I own even to you, my dear friend, that I
dreamed of the little girl, and Mr. Woodville's
wife ! and waked much hurried.

Has he a wife, I wonder !—ſhould he be un-
engaged, I fear your poor Emily's heart is in
danger. I muſt confeſs, I think I never ſaw ſo
pleaſing a man ; his voice is ſo like poor Harry's,
that it frequently made me ſtart ; but he ſpeaks
ſlower, and with ſome peculiar manner ; but
yet, the tone is muſic itſelf—but no more of
him—if he has a wife, I hope ſhe is as charming
as he is.

We had not quitted the breakfaſt table, when Mr. Herbert came in ; he ſtill looks the picture of ſorrow. Poor Lady Belmont had never ſeen him before ; ſhe could not ſtand it long ; I followed her Ladyſhip out of the room, and found her almoſt in hyſterics. After giving way to her heartrending feelings, ſhe begged I would prevent my Lord's expecting her to accompany us in our afternoon's viſit ; for till ſhe could better govern herſelf, ſhe found her ſpirits hurt, by throwing a gloom on the cheerfulneſs of others.

Mr. Herbert, in reſpect to her Ladyſhip, (whom he perceived his preſence had ſo much affected) would not ſtay dinner.

On my Lord's naming to him, his intention of viſiting his new neighbour this afternoon, Mr. Herbert ſaid, ' He is a very extraordinary cha' racter ; he arrived twelve days ago, in Mr. ' Ware's abſence ; who wrote to Mr. Gray, the

' worthy

' worthy minifter of the parifh, defiring he would
' introduce himfelf to Mr. Woodville, without
' ceremony ; but avoid afking any queftions, as
' he wifhed at prefent to be retired ; but wanted
' the acquaintance of a worthy divine, to affift
' him in the courfe of his prefent ftudy.

' Mr. Gray went the next morning, and was
' admitted, as foon as he fent in his name ; and
' has fince told me, he never was fo charmed
' with any man's converfation and behaviour in
' his life.

' He has been with him part of every day
' fince, and finds his admiration increafe each
' vifit. He fometimes ftays five hours at a time,
' inftructing him in the tenets of our religion,
' which he was very anxious to underftand tho-
' roughly ; telling Mr. Gray, till that neceffary
' point was gained, it was his choice to be as
' private as poffible ; he added, that he was born

' of

' of Christian parents, but had, from his early
' youth, lived in a land that knew not what was
' meaned by Christianity, nor had they books
' of any kind to instruct them. Yet, Mr. Gray
' says, he never conversed with any body who
' had more truly religious sentiments; a more
' honest heart, or more sound judgment, which
' guided a lively imagination. He seemed to be
' from nature, what others become from educa-
' tion; to be a philosopher, without learning;
' a hero without vice; and his mind to be like a
' garden, which produceth the sweetest flowers
' without weeds.

' His whole delight seems to be in a little girl;
' who is to be baptised, as soon as he believes
' himself sufficiently instructed in religion to ap-
' pear where he ought, to fulfil his own baptismal
' vow.

' All

All the time that is not spent with this en-
' gaging infant, he devotes to study : even in his
' walks, he reads ; for his pocket is always fur-
' nished with some useful book. His conversa-
' tion is lively and entertaining. Mr. Gray's
' account of him,' added Mr. Herbert, ' has
' made me much wish for his acquaintance.'

At five o'clock we set out, all very impatient
for a further knowledge of this wonderful man.

We stopped the coach, on beholding the most
pleasing object I ever saw. On the lawn, which
comes up to the parlour window, stood a neat
young female servant, by a tame lamb, dressed
with ribbands and flowers; and on the ground,
sat the loveliest child that ever I beheld, playing
with her equally innocent companion.

On our alighting, she jumped up, and with
an angelic sweetness, and vivacity ran to me.
I must give you an idea of the beautiful creature.—She is just three years old ; speaks plainer
than

than moſt children of that age—is finely formed—
has a lovely ſkin—freſh colour—ſweetly ſmiling
blue eyes—beautiful mouth—well ſhaped noſe—
and ſoft, ſhining dark brown hair ; her cap fell
off, as ſhe ran to me, as if unwilling to hide
one of thoſe pretty curls, which flowed in looſe
natural ringlets round her well-turned neck.

Her dreſs was a ſort of ſtays and coat, of fine
white calico ; over which, was a gown with ſhort
ſleeves, of white and ſilver gauze, faſtened acroſs
the ſtomach, with a broad black riband, buckled
by a ſmall buckle of large brilliants ; black ſhoes,
claſped with a very large diamond—Altogether,
the moſt delightful figure you ever beheld.

Think of the little angel running to me, and
holding up its pretty arms, ſaid, ' Pay, pay up.'
Indeed I took her up, and looked at her with a
tranſport that moiſtened my eyes ; which the ſweet
baby obſerving, and thinking there could be but
one cauſe for tears, ſtroaked my face, and ſaid,
' Don't cry, papa is better, and ſal be well ſoon.'

Whether

Whether Lady Anne envied me the pretty burthen I carried, I cannot fay; but fhe gave me one of her penetrating arch looks; however, I did not regard her, but carried my young friend in my arms, into the drawing-room; where we were received by Mr. and Mrs. Ware, and their fifter. Before we were feated, the gentleman entered; looking very pale, and his arm in a fling: the child left me, and ran to its father; he kiffed it, and bid the maid take it to walk.

After the ufual greetings, and civilities were over, the ftranger afked where Colonel Mandeville was?

My Lord informed him.—He fighed, and eagerly faid, ‘ When fhall I fee that moft ho-
‘ noured man ?’

Lord Belmont looked aftonifhment; and faid,
‘ Forgive me, fir, I do not mean to be imper-
‘ tinent; but every thing that relates to the man
‘ who preferved my life, muft be interefting to
‘ me—

' me—your impatience to see a stranger—the
' agitation I understand his letter to you occa-
' sioned—the seal on your reply to that letter;
' have, altogether, excited a curiosity in me,
' that I cannot suppress.'

The gentleman appeared embarrassed; after
a moment's pause, he answered, ' My Lord, I
' had determined not to divulge my name or situ-
' ation to any one, till I had seen Colonel Man-
' deville; but I think your Lordship's inter-
' cession may be of use to plead for me, to an
' injured parent! and the happy service I ren-
' dered you, may help to conceal the errors of—
' Charles Mandeville!'

My Lord started!

' Does your Lordship recollect a young kins-
' man of that name? I, my Lord, am that man;
' happy, or unhappy, as my father and you
' may receive me!'

My

My Lord, in a tranfport of joy, opened his arms, and embraced him in fpeechlefs rapture : at length, he faid, ' Oh, Charles ! welcome to ' my heart, and fortune !'

Mr. Mandeville received my Lord's careffes with delight, and refpect ; faying, ' Oh, fir ! ' be my friend; intercede for me with my of- ' fended father ! the blefling of his pardon will ' atone for many paft fufferings : I have great ' fears, that my receiving no anfwer to the few ' lines I fent him, penned in mifery, but fuf- ' ficiently explanatory ; is too plain a proof he ' does not mean to forgive his erring fon !'

' I will anfwer for him,' faid my Lord, ' that ' he has not received your letter, and that his ' joy only can exceed mine ; when I introduce ' to him fo worthy a man in his long loft child !' Then embracing him again, he added, ' May ' the divine mercy blefs you with mutual enjoy- ' ment of this unlooked for happinefs !'

' His

His Lordſhip wept ; and the ſpectators, who had ſat in ſilent wonder, joined their tears and congratulations : 'when my Lord ſaid, ' but ' pray, ſir, let me kiſs my pretty couſin, your ' ſweet infant !'

'The bell was rung ; and a ſervant entering, was ordered to fetch the little girl.

'Mr. Ware went out, and ſoon returned (followed by a ſervant with a ſalver of rich wines), ſaying, ' I know ladies, this is not cuſtomary ' before tea ; but I think ſuch intereſting ſub- ' jects require a more cordial refreſhment.' He took a glaſs, and preſented another to Lord Belmont ; requeſting we would all pledge him in drinking a happy meeting to Colonel Mandeville and his ſon. Every body followed the example with alacrity ; when Mr. Ware, turning to Lord Belmont, ſaid, he hoped he, and the ladies, would pardon any indecorum in his manner ; and

remember,

remember, trade, not politenefs, had been his
ftudy—he muft alfo intreat, that any farther difcourfe on the late interefting fubject, might be
poftponed for the prefent, on account of his
friend's weak ftate of health ; for though he had
recovered almoft miraculoufly, yet a relapfe might
be the confequence of too great agitation.'

My Lord approved the caution ; and turning
to Mr. Mandeville, faid, ' I hope, fir, you do
not feel yourfelf hurt ; affected, I fee you are.'

' Oh, my Lord! I am well; your kindnefs
' has lightened my heart—it has enabled me to
' look forward with a joy, that I have been long
' a ftranger to.'

Mr. Ware's defire was ftrictly adhered to ;
though, I dare fay, each party longed for more
information ; particularly, why all were in
mourning ; but the weepers worn by my Lord
and

and Mr. Mandeville, ſhowed the cauſe was too
ſerious, to admit of any enquiry.

I have written ſo much, I muſt now bid you
adieu !

EMILY HOWARD.

To Mifs KITTY FORTESCUE.

M Y good girl, you know, or at leaft you will,
I hope one day know, that when the die is caft,
and one is termed a bride elect, anxiety is over;
and one has the greater leifure to obferve other
people; now this being my cafe, I can fee, that
Emily fucceeds to my late thoughtful fituation;
however, as I have taken her pen, and fhall be
more honeft and minute in my detail than maiden
bafhfulnefs would permit her to be, I fhall leave
you to make your own comments; and affent
or not, to my opinion, as you fee caufe.

He (meaning Mr. Mandeville, for I fhall often
fay—he—to prevent repetitions; and, really,
there is fuch a noble dignity in his mien and air,
one would be apt to think there was no other he;)

is

is a ſtriking figure, though not delicately handſome.   I begin to think, it is well for ſomebody,
that my word was given before I ſaw this all-con-
quering hero,  for I fancy I ſhould prefer him ;  he
could ſo well entertain me with a world of anec-
dotes,  that would furniſh a never failing fund of
diſcourſe—no bad defence againſt dull domeſtic
hours ;  which, alas !  married people muſt expect ;  for even the beſt toned violins are not always in tune.

I find he has lived many years in a foreign
land ;  but how, or why he was there, we are yet
to learn.—He left the room,  for a few minutes,
which gave Mr. Ware the opportunity of informing us of this.

The ſervants entered with tea and coffee ;  and,
oh !  pretty ſight,  Mr. Mandeville followed, lead-
ing his lovely child,  holding a ſtraw baſket, filled
with toys ;  he carried the girl to my Lord, ſaying,  ‘ This is my real treaſure, though bleſt
‘ with an abundance of fortune.’

My

My Lord affectionately kissed the child; a tear of recollection fell down his cheeks; he wiped it off; sighed, and rising superior to selfish sorrow, said, with a cheerful air, 'It is a lovely 'infant; and, unless you give me a boy also, 'this pretty creature must be our heiress.'

Mr. Mandeville bowed; and sighing, said he had lost both his sons—this was his only child.

He then brought her to me, and then to Emily. The pretty innocent wished to sit in her lap; and in her broken language, said, 'how do oo do?' 'I have brought oo some pay things.'

The father gave a look of tenderness, which met a sympathetic spark in Emily's eyes; who, blushing, hung her head on the child's face. He said, 'My dear, have you no play things for 'any body else?'

The child answered, 'Yes, papa;' and then, as if she had been inspired, ran to her basket,

D                                          took

took out a fmall fillagree horfe, and flew with
it to Lord Belmont, faying, • 'There's a doold.
' horfe for oo, pay teep it.' Again fhe trotted
to the bafket, and choofing a bird, brought it
to me—' Here's a pitty bird for oo.' Again fhe
flew to her ftore, and came back to Emily, with.
a fmall, elegant filver figure, of exquifite work-
manfhip—' Here's a pitty man for oo.'

Emily took it, and blufhed fcarlet deep on
looking at it—but, goddefs of the defcriptive
powers affift me! how fhall I paint the joyful
father's countenance, at obferving the toy fhe
had chofen for Emily, and the blufhes it had
created in her ; for it was an image of himfelf ;
executed beyond any thing I ever faw : to heigh-
ten poor Emily's embarraffment, the child faid,
' Pray teep it for my fake.'

Emily, with artlefs cheerfulnefs, faid, ' I will,
' my fweet angel.'

                                    The

The father bowed—' Madam, you make me
' happy; the poor girl wants a friend, she has
' chosen one with a judgment superior to her
' age.'

Upon my word, I like this public fort of court-
ship; it is far more entertaining than the soft
nonsense generally made use of. I have a mind
to begin again, and teach my gentleman this new
mode of making love.

My Lord seemed to think it was high time to
relieve poor Emily, whose confusion was too vi-
sible ; so he took the image saying, that, it was
too rich, and curious a gift for a child to make ;
but that he would deposit it in his cabinet of cu-
riosities.

I thought, I observed his Lordship's speech cast
a gloom over Mr. Mandeville's features.

General chat ensued; but no one, I find,
says one word of poor Mrs. Ware, and her

sister.—

fiſter.—Well then, they are civil, well-meaning, good ſort of women ; neither handſome or plain ; behaved juſt as they ought, and played the under parts of the drama very well.

The heat of the room made Mr. Ware propoſe a walk, when tea was over.

My Lord ſaid, if the grounds were as much improved as the houſe, ſince he had ſeen them, he ſhould be greatly gratified by viewing them ; but that he would firſt order the coach, leſt a late hour ſhould give Lady Belmont an unneceſſary alarm.

Mr. Mandeville replied, he was glad to hear her Ladyſhip named—his Lordſhip's dreſs had precluded any enquiry after her.

My Lord ſighed bitterly, and ſhowed he was much affected ; but conquering himſelf once more, we all roſe, and proceeded to the garden. The gentlemen (according to the abominable

Angloiſe

Angloife fafhion) foon left us poor women to the dull chat of a female vifit.

When it was near eight o'clock, the fervants informed us the coach was ready; the gentlemen were approaching near enough for me to obferve my Lord take off his finger the fine family ring he always wears, and fo highly values, and put it on Mr. Mandeville's finger.

Proper civilities ended, we got into the carriage—every body filent—the women all impatient to hear, but my Lord kept in compofed meditation for near half the way; at length he faid, ' I have been reflecting, Lady Anne, on the ' wonderful work of Providence in this affair. ' My friend never was near fo fond of this fon, ' as of poor Harry. Charles was as promifing ' a lad as his brother, but lefs tractable; and had ' a fpirit that would not fubmit to correction.— ' He ran away from fchool, becaufe, he faid, ' he would not be whipped like a dog or a flave.

' -After

'After this event, we had every reason to
'suppose him lost in the Victory. The Colonel's
'exceffive fondness for his youngest son, made
'him, perhaps, too soon reconcile himself to
'the loss of the eldest; who, now you see, is
'preferved to comfort and alleviate his sorrow,
'and be the support of his age.

'Happy Colonel! I have no child!' He paufed—sighed heavily—then, with an animated
voice, said, 'Yes, Charles must be as a son
'to me; I did not give him life, but he has
'preferved mine. The little girl too—oh, my
'Julia! how like thy tender age. Well, Hea-
'ven be praised, my friends are happier than
'myself!'

He stopped again, and then said, 'I am
'furprised to find fo fine an understanding, in a
'man who can have seen fo little of the world—
'can have had fo few advantages; he has not
'even had the common affiftance of books.'

The

The coachman drove up the ſweep ; my Lady, who had been watching anxiouſly for her Lord's ſafe return, met us at the drawing-room door. He immediately told her, he had received much ſatisfaction from his viſit, and hoped he ſhould make her partake of it—adding, ' This day has ' given pleaſure, even to me !'

Lady Belmont ſighed, and ſaid ſhe was glad to hear it.

' Do you not,' ſaid my Lord, ' recollect Char- ' les Mandeville ?'

' To be ſure I do ; he was always my favorite, ' though not his father's ; the child, too, was ' much fonder of me than his brother was : poor ' fellow, why mention him now ?'

' In order to give your Ladyſhip the pleaſure ' of hearing, this loſt boy—this beloved Charles, ' was the preſerver of my life, at the hazard of ' his own. He really is the agreeable man Mr. ' Herbert

' Herbe.t defcribed this morning, Mr. Ware
' hirgs him to-morrow, with his only child, a
' very beautiful little girl, to pay his refpects to
' your Ladyfhip.'


' Is is poffible ?' faid Lady Belmont.  ' Do I
' owe my deareft Lord's life to that fweet boy ?
' Blefs him, gracious Heaven !  How fhall I love
' and thank him ?  Is he quite recovered?'


' Almoft ; and entirely by the ufe of thofe
' herbs he brought from a diftant country, in
' which he lived fo long ; he feems very partial
' to it ; he will not allow it to be uncivilized,
' becaufe tainted with no vice.—Its natives give
' way to the natural dictates of benevolence.


' He means to fpend fome time with us at
' Belmont.'   (Here Emily's eyes brightened.)
' So as this houfe caufed the Colonel's affliction,
' here I hope to heal his forrows, by reftoring
' to him a long loft fon.—A fine fellow too,  is
' well made—has the air of a monarch—natu-
                                        ' rally

' rally well complexioned, but now rather fun-
' burnt ; but his features are fo agreeable, one
' does not mind his fkin ; he has fine teeth, a
' pleafing mouth, a good nofe, and very fine
' intelligent eyes.   His afpect befpeaks courage
' and humanity ; I confefs, I am much pleafed
' with him.—I begin to think I have erred, in
' fuppofing it neceffary to take fo much pains
' to educate a young man.

' Here is one, who has no claffical knowledge
' —has not been taught the Graces ; and yet,
' one can difcover no deficiency either in his
' converfation, or his manner.'.

I joined in his praifes, with my ufual warmth.
Emily faid little, but in that little, it was eafy
to difcover her opinion was as much in his favor,
at leaft, as thofe who had fpoken more copioufly.

I was called out, and learned my fervant had
returned in our abfence with the letter I had fent

to

to Colonel Mandeville; hearing in town, that the Colonel had not ſtopped longer at his own houſe than was neceſſary to change horſes; but had gone to his ſick friend, with all poſſible expedition; and had left word, that he ſhould not return through London, but be at Belmont in a few days.

Poor agitated man! he had forgotten to order the letter, he had deſired me to ſend after him, ſhould be forwarded to his friend's houſe; ſo my ſervant thought it better to bring it back to me.

As I hate concealments—alas, have they not been fatal to this family!—and ſaw no reaſon for keeping Lord Belmont a ſtranger now, to the ſtory of the watch, I returned to the drawing-room, with the packet in my hand; and informed them of that tranſaction; adding, that as the event was ſo doubtful, I thought it more prudent not to agitate his Lordſhip's mind, by ſurmiſes, that might prove falſe.

My

My Lord kindly faid, ' Confiderate Lady
' Anne !' There, who could have thought I
fhould have ever deferved that epithet ?

We talked the reft of the evening, with a
cheerfulnefs that has long been banifhed from our
converfation in this houfe ; and Lady Belmont
went to her apartment with a livelier, afpect than
fhe has had fince her heavy affliction.

How amiable does her mind, and my Lord's
appear on this occafion; thus fharing in the joy
which others have—on a fubject too, from which
they are for ever precluded knowing joy ; for,
alas ! there can never be another Lady Julia !
Adieu !

To

To Lady ANNE WILMOTT.

AT laft, the difagreeable bufinefs is finifhed—
difagreeable, becaufe it has detained me from
the beft beloved of my heart !—May I not hope,
that as the time of meeting draws near, you, alfo,
feel an increafe of impatience ?

I have executed your Ladyfhip's orders, in regard to Mifs Haftings ; and, I flatter myfelf,
in a manner that will gain the approbation of
the moft generous of female hearts !

In

In a few days then, I truſt to receive the bright reward of my long ſuffering; reading in your animated countenance, that you ſhare in the happineſs that our meeting will give

Your faithful

EDWARD BELVILLE.

To Mr. Herbert.

Sir,

THOUGH ſtocked with a tolerable ſhare of levity, yet, when I give my feelings time to operate, I love to endeavour to alleviate the ſufferings of others: accept this eulogy on myſelf, as an apology for the liberty I take in writing to you; as I am convinced, your knowing that the happy event in this family, has ſoftened their ſore affliction, will ſooth your grief for the loſs of your friend——a true friend he was to every body, except himſelf. But to my ſubject.——You have heard the preface to my tale.

This day we expected Mr. Mandeville, to dinner; but, at two o'clock, came Mr. Ware alone; he immediately calmed our fears for his friend, by aſſuring us he was very well, and very

happy;

happy; and, with a fmiling countenance, prefented my Lord with a letter. On obferving that
we females were going to retire, and judging, I
fuppofe, that as daughters of Eve, we were not
wholly without curiofity, he faid, ' I am cer-
' tain there can be no occafion for the ladies'
' abfence; all here are too much interefted in
' what concerns Mr. Mandeville, to make con-
' cealment neceffary.' My Lord then read
aloud—

' Your Lordfhip's benevolent difpofition, en-
' fures my pardon for a greater omiffion than de-
' ferring, for a few hours, the honor of waiting
' on your Lordfhip, and Lady Belmont. I have
' feen my father, and am his happy fon, and
 ' Your Lordfhip's
  ' Obedient humble fervant,
   ' CHARLES MANDEVILLE, Jun.'

Lord Belmont requefted to hear the particulars
of this defirable meeting.

        Mr.

Mr. Ware faid, ' I am an early rifer, and
' was employed in writing a letter to your Lord-
' fhip, by way of cover to fome papers, relative
' to Mr. and Mrs. Mandeville. She, poor wo-
' man, gave them into my hands a few days be-
' fore her death; and, in a very affecting man-
' ner, faid——

' If you ever meet with a friend that loves my
' Charles, give him thefe papers; I would not
' truft them with him; knowing his innate mo-
' defty would rather fupprefs the truths they tell
' fo much to his honor; and would never divulge
' to his friends, that he has been the glory, I
' may almoft fay, the idol of a whole nation, and
' of two neighbouring kingdoms.'

My Lord eagerly cried out, ' Sir, give them
' to me——they are my right——I claim them
' as fuch, as I truly love the man.'

Mr. Ware then produced a large packet, and
was going to unfeal it.

' Do

' Do not open it now,' faid my Lord; ' I
' will perufe them in my ftudy.'

Mr. Ware replied, he was only going to take
out the letter he had taken the liberty to write;
which was unneceffary now he was himfelf the
bearer of them.

' Oh, pray let me fee your letter, it will affift
' me, I dare fay, in underftanding the memoirs,
' and in forming my judgment.—I beg you will
' proceed with a relation of the affecting inter-
' view.'

Mr. Ware prefented the packet, unopened,
and faid, ' Juft as I had fealed my letter, Mr.
' Mandeville entered, faying, he hoped he had
' not detained me from breakfaft; but he had
' been preparing for a longer expedition than to
' Belmont; as he intended fetting off to Lon-
' don, the moment he had paid his refpects to
' Lady Belmont, in hopes of feeing his father.

' We

‘ We had more difcourfe, and I, by degrees,
‘ unfolded to him the misfortunes in his family ;
‘ which I had learned laft night from Mr Gray,
‘ who called foon after your Lordfhip went, and
‘ did not fee Mr. Mandeville ; as I had pre-
‘ vailed on him to go to bed, after the agitation
‘ his mind had been in.

‘ I thought it right to inform him of thofe
‘ particulars, left by fome painful queftions, he
‘ might diftrefs a fond parent.’

Mr. Ware proceeded, without feeming to obferve the uneafinefs his difcourfe occafioned
here.

‘ I was reafoning him into compofure, when
‘ we heard a carriage ftop. The fervant enquir-
‘ ed for me ; and a gentleman alighted, juft as
‘ I had reached the hall door ; with an agitated
‘ voice, he faid, ‘ I am glad, fir, to fee you fo
‘ well recovered.’

‘ I told

' I told him it was my friend that had been
' hurt, and that I had not been ill.

' Obſerving his dreſs, it that moment ſtruck
' me, he was Colonel Mandeville.——I led him,
' therefore, a longer road into the breakfaſt-
' parlour, to give Mr. Mandeville time to re-
' tire, which I knew he would do, on the ap-
' proach of company.

' My ſcheme anſwered, for we found the room
' empty ; when the gentleman ſaid, ' Pray in-
' troduce me to the preſerver of Lord Belmont's
' life, my name is Mandeville.'—' I will look,
' ſir, if he is in the ſtudy ; but I ſuſpect he is
' walked out.'

' I went to my wife, begging of her to haſten
' breakfaſt, and leave us, as ſoon as it was fi-
' niſhed. Next, I went to Mr. Mandeville, and
' requeſted I might ſend his chocolate to his dreſ-
' ſing-room ; as I had a perſon with me about
' buſineſs.

'I then

' I then returned to the parlour, followed by
' my wife and the child; who being accuftomed
' to ftrangers, ran up to the newly arrived.

' Sir, faid I, you have probably come a long
' way this morning, pleafe to take fome refrefh-
' ment, whilft they are fearching for my friend.

' He took up the little girl, faying, ' This is
' a lovely child; mifs, may I kifs you ?' She
' turned up her fmiling face, and he was fo plea-
' fed with her, that he faid, ' God blefs you,
' you are a delightful girl !'

' He eat a bit of roll, and drank a cup of cho-
' colate; declining any more, and growing
' plainly impatient, I looked at my wife, who
' retired with the child.

' I then turned to Colonel Mandeville, fay-
' ing, ' The gentleman you enquire for, will
' come as foon as I inform him you are here;
' but I chofe you fhould take fome refrefhment
                                    ' firft,

' firſt, as he has ſome very intereſting intelli-
' gence for you.—He knows, that a ſon of your's,
' whom you have ſuppoſed loſt in the Victory,
' is alive, and well.'

' What do you ſay, ſir ? Is my Charles Man-
' deville living.'

' Yes, ſir ; and to convince you, he ſent a
' watch and ſeal to be ſhewn you when there was
' an opportunity ; which it ſeems accident con-
' veyed to you the other night.'

' Oh, merciful God ! have I ſtill a ſon ? Oh,
' ſir ! let me embrace the man who knows my
' Charles !'

' I went out to prepare my friend, but I had
' no ſooner named his father, than he bruſhed
' by me and flew down ſtairs with ſuch rapidity,
' that when I had gotten to the parlour, I found
' his father trembling in an arm chair, and
' Mr.

' Mr. Mandeville on his knees, holding his
' hand, and calling loudly for water and drops.

' At length, the Colonel found utterance for
' his raptures, and said, ' I am well, my child,
' I am indeed ;' and embracing his son, shed a
' plentiful shower of tears. Then turning to
' me, ' Oh, sir ! it was well you had prepared
' me, or excefs of joy had finished what excefs
' of grief had not done.'

' The son was feeling his father's pulse, whilst
' the tears streamed down his manly cheeks.—
' Oh, sir ! do you indeed forgive me ?'

' Yes, my child ; as truly as I hope to be
' forgiven.' He then bleffed him, and said,
' May you live long, and happily ! Merciful
' Heaven ! how happy am I, when I thought
' all comfort had fled for ever !'

' Mr. Mandeville went haftily out of the room,
' and returning with the child in his arms, pla-
' ced

' ced it on its knees before the Colonel; faying,
' Blefs this dear infant too; fhe is mine!'

' I bleffed her, before I knew fhe was your's;
' again, I pray to Heaven to pour down bleffings
' on her;' and kiffing it cordially, the poor
' thing looked frightened, and ftretched out her
' pretty arms to her father.

' The Colonel faid, ' Take it in your lap,
' and fit before me, that I may gaze with delight
' on you both.——Have you not a fon for me
' alfo?'

' No, fir, this little darling is all I pof-
' fefs.'

' The Colonel, plainly miftaking his mean-
' ing, faid, ' Child, I have not much cafh
' about me; but (taking out his pocket book)
' here is a hundred pound note for the prefent;
' and I think I know how to provide for the fu-
' ture.'

                                        ' Mr.

' Mr. Mandeville took it refpectfully; and
' fmiling, faid, ' Oh, fir, you muft be fo good
' as to affift my friend Mr. Ware, in fettling
' my affairs, for I am but a novice in thefe mat-
' ters; and am poffeffed of more wealth than I
' know what to do with.'

' You are a novice, indeed, child, to fay fo;
' but a fhort refidence in England, will foon
' make you change your opinion; and find the
' elegance and luxury of the prefent age, will
' require a large ftore of riches. I have heard
' of nothing but the arrival of two fhips, im-
' menfely freighted, configned to a Mr. Ware.
' I hope, fir, you are the fortunate owner of
' them.'

' I am the man, fir, faid I, they are configned
' to; but I am only your fon's agent; the cargo
' is his, and I fhall gain enough by the com-
' miffion.'

' Give me leave, fir,' faid Mr. Mandeville,
' to

‘ to entreat you will take this little pocket-book ;
‘ I believe it contains notes to about twelve thou-
‘ fand pounds value ;  as an earneſt of our future
‘ proſperity.’

‘ Oh ! it is too, too much for an old man ;
‘ were it not for the recollection of my dear
‘ Harry, I ſhould feel too much joy—but there,
‘ my heart muſt ever bleed ! however, no more
‘ of thoſe thoughts now ; it ſeems ungrateful to
‘ Providence, who has thus wonderfully bleſſed
‘ me ! I had determined, within theſe few mi-
‘ nutes, to ſell my commiſſion, to ſecure a ſup-
‘ port for that dear little one!’

‘ In ſhort, it is impoſſible to repeat the ten-
‘ derneſs which filled their hearts, and over-
‘ flowed in their words.

‘ I then mentioned the appointment at Bel-
‘ mont ; ſaying, I imagined it would be more
‘ agreeable to them to wait till after dinner ;

E                          ‘ and

' and that I would go and inform your Lordſhip
' of this happy meeting, and leave the gentle-
' men to follow in the afternoon.'

We all expreſſed our happineſs---Lady Belmont, with her uſual politeneſs, thanked Mr.
Ware for his attention to her friends.

I am certain you will receive pleaſure in hearing a Charles is found, to comfort this family;
though he can never be to your heart, ſo dear as
was the lively engaging Harry !

I am, &c.

ANNE WILMOTT.

To

To Mifs KITTY FORTESCUE.

I FIND Emily has given you a copious detail of the joyful meeting of the father and fon; and I have forbidden her to proceed with her account, as, from fome caufe or other, fhe has a violent head-ach; and, in obedience to my royal orders, is laid down, in hopes to regain her good looks before the afternoon——*entre nous,* I think then, fhe would be forry not to wear her beft face; and as eafe of mind, and health of body, are all fhe requires to affift her native charms; we will try for that delightful rouge they can produce——Warren's milk of rofes is nothing to it !

You fee, therefore, you muft be content with

E 2

my

my pen; or remain ignorant of ten thoufand things, you want to know.

After dinner, my Lord requefted us females to entertain Mr. Ware, as he was anxious to perufe the papers, before he faw Mr. Mandeville again; fo retired to his ftudy.—I confefs, I wifhed he had ordered me to be of his party.

At that inftant, the door opened, and my heart leaped to meet its long-loved mafter! I flew to receive him, and conduct him into another. parlour, leaving the company to laugh at me, as I formerly fhould have done at any perfon in the fame foolifh fituation.

When we had enjoyed a little tête-à-tête, we joined the party in the drawing-room; and my Belville paid his compliments, with that grace, which, if you credit my judgment, accompanies all his words and actions.

Pray

Pray do not fuppofe that nobody is to be admired and praifed, but this fame Indian ftranger !

Tea over, we went into the garden ; but not till I had ftolen up to Emily ; I found her dreffing herfelf with an elegance that fhewed her head was well ; whatever her heart might be !

My beloved companion and I, foon preferred a fhady feat ; which neither thought of quitting till hearing voices near us, we looked up, and faw the company approaching, and increafed by my Lord, the Colonel and his fon.

We immediately joined them, and I prefented Belville ; and taking out of my pocket, the letter I had inclofed to Colonel Mandeville, delivered it to him ; wifhing him joy of the happy explanation.

‘ I have joy indeed, oh, Lady Anne, I am ‘ bleffed beyond the power of words to exprefs !’

On

On our return to the house, we met the blush-ing Emily ; she paid her proper compliments to the gentlemen, with that sweet timidity, which accompanies all she does ; but on this particular occasion, seemed rather more embarrassing to herself, than usual.

' I watched Mr. Mandeville's tell-tale eyes; and saw they were brightened with pleasure.   Mr. Ware went home before supper, as his sister-in-law's  having  a  bad cold prevented  his wife's accompanying the Colonel and Mr. Mandeville.

Supper passed over more cheerfully than any I have seen here for a long time ; and before I retired to my own room, I determined to  have some chat with Emily ; but she spoiled my scheme of teazing her a little by her artless sincerity ; for as soon as I remarked that Mr. Mandeville seem-ed to ' hang over her' as Milton says, ' de-' lighted with looks of cordial love :' she with great ingenousness said, ' I confess, Lady Anne, ' till I saw Mr. Mandeville, I never formed a
                                                    ' wish

' wish for marriage; but I own with that since-
' rity which is due to you; I should be happy to
' be united to that amiable man. But my dear
' Madam, be still my friend : assist me to con-
' quer this too forward partiality for one I know
' so little of; one too, who may have views of
' a very different nature !—I see my error, teach
' me to correct it.'

I assured her I would, when I found it necessary. Her franknefs has more than ever endea-
red her to me; and I will assist her ; more however, according to the real wishes of her heart,
than her request implies.

I wished her a good night ; and shall do the
fame by you.---For as this is Saturday, we must
rise early to-morrow, to prepare for church.
Adieu !

ANNE WILMOTT.

To

To Mr. HERBERT.

YOUR polite reply to my laſt, indulges me in the very thing I wanted, by finding a channel for my thoughts to flow into; for they really crowd ſo faſt, they want room.

Your abſence from this part of the country, juſt at this time, therefore, though it deprives you of the pleaſure of witneſſing ſome intereſting ſcenes, is, you ſee, very uſeful to me; but you moſt forgive incoherencies, and inconſiſtencies; I was always addicted to them : the ſtrange events that have happened here within this week (and why ſhould I not own the arrival of a certain per-ſon, of ſome importance to me) have not proved great regulators of my irregular ideas; and I am but juſt able to recollect, that we all aſſem-
bled

bled this morning before church time ; when the little pratler (who arrived before breakfaſt, as did Mr. Mandeville's ſervants, clothes, &c.  as this is to be his home) told us, ſhe was to go ſome day, to have her face waſhed at church.   This her anxious father has told her, to prevent her being frightened at that  part of the ceremony, when ſhe is chriſtened.

Suppoſe us at the church ; where I never had ſeen the Colonel ſo devout before.—Aſtoniſhment and pleaſure beamed in his face, when the clergyman ſaid, with  an audible voice, juſt before the thankſgiving,  ' Charles Mandeville, junior, ' deſires to  return moſt  humble. and  hearty ' thanks,  for his  happy return. to .his native: ' land.---'

I am aſhamed to ſay, I ſuſpected our new found friend  was tinged with methodiſm.   Thus I fell into the too common error,  of thinking a diſplay of  more religion  than appears neceſſary,  or is cuſtomary, is hypocriſy : however a converſation

E 3                    in

in the afternoon, made me fee my fault ; and as a punifhment, I own it to you.

After dinner, as the child was fitting in Lady Belmont's lap, her Ladyfhip faid to Mr. Mandeville, ' I am going to afk a favour of you, ' fir.'——

' I am pretty fure your Ladyfhip can afk no-' thing but what will reflect honor upon me, to ' comply with.'

' It is, to be fponfor, when this pretty crea-' ture is made a chriftian.'

' I,' faid the Colonel, ' muft infift on being ' the god father, as my right.'

' Then,' faid I, ' unlefs I take Lady Ma-' ry's place, I requeft to be the other god-mo-' ther.'——

Mr.

Mr. Mandeville gracefully bowed to us all; and said, ' It was gratifying his utmoft wifh, ' fo to honor his dear little Indian; and I hope ' to call upon you foon. For I flatter myfelf, fir, turning to his father, ' you will permit me to ' accompany you, next Sunday, to the facra- ' ment; when I have obeyed our Saviour's laft ' injunction, it will complete my happinefs to ' carry my child to be received into his flock.'

The Colonel replied---' Be not fo precipitate, ' Charles, in matters of religion; let your ' daughter be baptized—to be fure that fhould ' not be delayed; but as to the other part, it ' is time enough, when your king and country ' call upon you, to prove your faith.'

' I find you think me too hafty, fir; but Mr. ' Gray has taken much pains and trouble to in- ' ftruct me in my duty; and he has given me ' great fatisfaction, by affuring me, I need not ' longer poftpone a thing I fo ardently defire. ' Your judgment ought to guide mine, but that

' you

' you may be the better able to form it, I will
' unfold my fentiments, and lay before you the
' plan I formed on my arrival in England.


' Firft, to ftudy the Chriftian Religion in its
' native purity; then to feek out you, fir, and
' try to obtain your bleffing; obferving all the
' time, to difcharge my duty, in due care of my
' dear wife's pledge of true love: thus, when I
' had endeavoured to make myfelf lefs unworthy,
' to hope for a bleffing from Heaven upon all
' my actions, by a confcience free from felf re-
' proach—then---and not till then, to turn my
' mind to fuch ftudies, as would make me a
' worthy member of this country; fuch as would
' be no difgrace to my friends here, nor to the
' country in which I had received my education;
' where, if I had acquired no learning, I had
' feen no vice; or at leaft, as little as frail na-
' ture will permit us to know.


' I efteem it no fmall comfort, to gain the
' bleffings of the poor, therefore I have tried to
' relieve

' relieve every diſtreſs I have heard of; and I
' hope it will not be thought vanity in me, when
' I declare, I have endeavoured to fulfil every
' branch of my duty, as faſt as I have learned
' them.

' Time will, I truſt, make me more perfect;
' and in the mean while, I hope I ſhall be par-
' doned the errors that ariſe from ignorance.

' What may I not hope for? bleſſed with a
' forgiving parent, who pardons the fault that
' has ſo long lain heavy on my conſcience; and
' with the example of ſuch friends as ſurround
' me!---And as to the goods of fortune, I have
' wealth, more than enough, to ſatisfy the moſt
' ambitious man!—

' Wonder not then, my deareſt ſir, that I am
' impatient to give every proof of my gratitude
' to the giver of all good, for his mercies to
' me!'—

The

The Father could contain no longer, but in a voice of rapture, called out, ‘ Oh, Charles, my ‘ deareſt ſon; thou art every way my ſupe- ‘ rior !’

‘ Do not, ſir, ſo confound me by praiſes I ‘ cannot merit, but rectify my errors; then, ‘ with an heart at eaſe, I can apply to proper ‘ ſtudies; and hope to make myſelf in time, a ‘ uſeful member of my native land; never forget- ‘ ting to ſerve, when I can, its caſt off Colony, ‘ in the northern part of India’

‘ I find,’ ſaid Lord Belmont, ‘ the beſt edu- ‘ cation is to be well inſtructed in virtue.’

‘ A virtuous mind, ſir, is certainly the beſt ‘ ſoil for inſtruction-- keep out the rubbiſh of ‘ vice, and there will be no impediment to the ‘ fair growth of juſtice; which I conſider as ‘ the main root, from whence all the other vir- ‘ tues ſhoot; and without which, there can, ac-
‘ cording

' cording to my notion, be no fuch thing as true
' virtue.'


' Surely,' faid Colonel Belville, ' you have
' lived with a race of philofophers !'


' Not fo, fir; they know neither the word,
' or its meaning ; neither have they any books,
' excepting four fmall ones, written in a lan-
' guage, neither they nor I could read. They
' have very little idea of any religion ; but the
' little they have learned, has been continued by
' tradition (without any addition or alteration,
' they believe) from one generation to another,
' for upwards of four hundred years; and is
' ftrictly adhered to.'


Lady Belmont faid, ' You mentioned it as
' your opinion, that they were a caft off colony
' —from what nation ?'


' From England, madam, I am inclined to
' think, for many reafons --firft, their language,
' though

' though materially different from ours, has
' such a resemblance in the sound, and is so ex-
' actly the same in some words, that I soon learn-
' ed it, and they very soon acquired mine ; per-
' haps, neither were very correct ; but each
' soon understood the other, without difficulty,

' They worshipped one supreme Deity—the
' invisible God of heaven and earth ; and all the
' ritual they had, was the Lord's prayer, the
' creed, and the ten commandments ; which
' were very nearly the same as ours :---the repea-
' ting these, and singing hymns, is their only
' form of worship. From these, they formed
' their laws, which none infringed, without in-
' curring sure disgrace.'

The Colonel said, ' I suppose their punish-
' ments were very severe.'

No, sir ; they would not appear so in our
' country :——murder is the only crime that is
' punished

' punifhed with death; and very feldom was it
' committed.

' Their rewards are, an increafe of honor;
' their punifhments, difgrace; which, in gene-
' ral, is as much dreaded as death.

' For a known, a wilful falfity, the firft of-
' fence was punifhed by difgrace; the fecond, by
' banifhment, for what length of time the fupe-
' rior choofes.—They are fent away to a dif-
' tance, in a very large boat, which is to be
' ftored with whatever they choofe to carry with
' them. At the appointed time of their return,
' they are received in a very friendly manner;
' and every hint of reproach ftrictly prohibited;
' and fo they often become worthy members of
' the community. In all the time I lived there,
' there was occafion to banifh only two perfons,
' —one of them came fafe back, and is now a
' very worthy man.'

' Pray,'

' Pray,' faid Colonel Mandeville, what do you
' mean by difgrace ? and if they have no laws,
' how can they be faid to deferve it ?'

' Sir, they have rules—to difobey them, is to
' deferve difgrace---to explain the nature of that
' difgrace, I muft inform you, nobody has any
' power there, but what age entitles him to ;
' therefore age is their ambition ; and this is to
' be gained by merit ; or loft by demerit.'

' What, fir, can they make a man older or
' younger, as they think proper ?'

' Yes, fir ; and nobody has any property of
' any kind, but what the ftate allows, accord-
' ing to his rank ; which is determined entirely
' by the age they have voted him to be of.'

' Pray, Charles, how old was you ?'

' I was fixty, and unanimoufly offered to be
' feventy.'

' How

‘ How old when you firſt went ?’

‘ They allowed me no age at all; I was, in
‘ their eſtimation, the loweſt perſon there.’

‘ What do you ſay ?——not a ſlave, I hope.’

‘ There is no ſuch thing in the country; nor
‘ have they the ſmalleſt idea what ſlavery means.
‘ My ſmall knowledge of European cuſtoms,
‘ makes me a bad defender of the rules, diſpo-
‘ ſition, and ſtrict integrity of thoſe worthy In-
‘ dians; but a whole race with more virtue, or
‘ leſs vice, I really believe cannot be found upon
‘ earth.’

‘ Well,’ ſaid the Colonel, ‘ I muſt not call
‘ a ſon older than myſelf, child.’

‘ To my ear it would not ſound extraordinary,
‘ as I have ſeen many a father his ſon’s junior;
‘ for a perſon of an indolent temper, without ambition, may live ſixty, ſeventy, or eighty
‘ ſprings,

' springs, without attaining any age; and one
' who has not feen thirty fprings, may attain to
' fixty, or feventy years of age, which none can
' exceed.'

' So then you have been the eldeft man in the
' country.'

' No, fir; I was offered to be fo, but I did
' not think myfelf a proper object for fo high an
' honor.'

Pray, fir,' faid I, ' how do they determine
' as to the women? I fhould fuppofe the giving
' them twenty or thirty years, would be no great
' incitement to virtuous actions; but, perhaps
' they reverfe it, and take years from them.'

Mr. Mandeville fmiled, and faid, There have
' been very few. inftances, madam, of the wo-
' men attaining any age at all.'

, ' Oh, fir, your fervant; I am anfwered.'

' Do

' Do not, however, miſtake me, madam,
' and infer, that they think meanly of the ſex
' —it would be doing great injuſtice; but the
' feminine merit is confined to the duties of do-
' meſtic life; and it has been very rarely known,
' that any woman deviated from the general man-
' ner of life, ſo as to be claſſed amongſt the can-
' didates for age: yet, were the honor to be
' conferred on them, for private virtues, few
' countries could ſhew more exemplary inſtances
' of good wives, and amiable mothers, than I
' have ſeen there.'

He ſighed heavily, and I was ſorry my flip-
pancy had probed a wound, hardly healed
yet.

My Lord interrupted Mr. Mandeville's reflections, by ſaying, ' I have been ſo entertained
' with the account of my countrymen in India;
' and pleaſed with the proofs I have read of their
' honeſt ſimplicity, and of the high affection
' they had for you; that I muſt enquire if you
'' ever

' ever repented leaving England ; I fhould fup-
' pofe you did not, by the information I have
' received of your being fo greatly beloved,  and
' fo greatly honored by a wife,  and virtuous peo-
' ple ;  whofe judgments were directed by native
' truth,  candour,  and honefty.


   ' I can affure the  company, that Mr. Man-
' deville  attained  the  highest  honor,  and most
' juftly deferved the  title  of—honorable---which
' they beftow only upon exalted merit.'


His Honor looked abafhed,  but not  daunted ;
then,  with a becoming dignity,  replied, ' True,
' I was fo  rewarded,  for  fome fervices I was  fo
' happy as to render thefe noblest encouragers of
' virtue ;  and for their credit,  and my own,  will
' not difguife my fentiments.    . . .


   ' I never did repent leaving my  tyrannical
' fchool-mafter,  who whipped me  as if I had
' been a flave ; for faults too,  that I did not
                      ' commit ;

commit; and charged me with falfehoods I
' had never uttered.

' You muft remember, fir,' turning to his fa-
' ther, ' my complaining to you of his harfh
' treatment; you replied, I muft go through
' the fchool difcipline——fupplied me with mo-
' ney, which enabled me to purchafe candles
' to add part of the night to my hours of ftudy;
' and moft luckily (as it has proved) gave me
' that watch, which you knew again.

' One night, that I was particularly anxious
' to excel my form in verfes, (having, by your
' defire, been abfent from fchool the day before
' they were to be given up) I was obliged to fit
' up till paft two o'clock, to complete my tafk.

' This made me unufually fleepy in the morn-
' ing. A boy, as he went by my room, called,
' and found me in bed; and fnatching my watch
' off the table, ran away.

I flipped

' I flipped on my clothes, and after a scuffle,
' recovered my watch.—My master catched us
' in the fray, which had detained us both too
' long from school.  I was called up, but begged
' lea e first to go  for my task, which I had left
' in my other coat pocket.

'  .  · excuse for idleness, sir.'

'          no excuse, sir;  give me leave to send
'  ..

' No,  I dare say you have not got it ready—
' I am certain you lie.'

' Sir,  I should scorn to lie, whatever you may
' think of me.'

' Ah!  you are saucy, are you ;  I shall make
' you suffer for it, assure yourself.'

' He  then  called  up the other boy ;  a bigger
                              · ' boy,

' boy, but not a better fcholar—afked him, what
' had been the caufe of our quarrel.

' He replied, ' Mandeville was late in bed,
' and on his hearing he would be too late for
' fchool, grew furly, fo we quarreled.'

' Did you not take his watch?
' Yes, fir; but it was out of jeft, and he has
' it again."

' Well, I hope you have not negleﬅed your
' talk to-day, as you did yefterday.'

' No, fir; but in the fighting I loft it out of
' my pocket.'

' Fye, fye, go your way, and be more care-
' ful hereafter.'———' Now fir,' turning to me,
' I will give you a few ftrokes for telling me an
' untruth, and for your faucinefs.'

' He was as good as his word; and whipped
' me fo cruelly, I was not able to walk; and
' for two days kept my bed.

F

' This

' This manifeſt injuſtice would not let me
' ſleep at night, or have peace in the day ; and
' I reſolved rather to die, than continue in the
' power of ſuch a tyrant.

' As I was beloved by my ſchool-fellows, I
' was pitied by moſt of them. I had one fa-
' vorite, a little older than myſelf, to him I told
' my mind.

' He ſaid, if I could get healed enough to go
' off with him, in three days, when he went
' to the Victory, where his brother was a lieu-
' tenant, and he was himſelf to be a midſhip-
' man, he had no doubt but he could prevail
' on the captain to take me ; as he was ſure he
' could anſwer for it, I was not a coward.

' I replied, no, no ; with fair play, I feared
' nothing. In ſhort, we managed ſo well, that
' all my wearables were packed in his box ; and
' it was late when he took his leave ; and I lock-
' ed my chamber door, and contrived to ſteal
' out, a little time before him.

' We

. ' We met at the appointed fpot—took a poft
' chaife to Greenwich ; and then took boat, and
' went off to the fhip.

' The captain being informed of my arrival,
' afked who I was ? and why I came thither ?

' At this moment, I determined to change
' my name, to that of Woodville ; which, as
' it was my mother's, I thought I had an equal
' right to—which I flattered myfelf, would pre-
' vent any difcredit to my family, for the ftep I
' had taken, and alfo fcreen me from being
' difcovered, if enquired for ; I anfwered the
' captain, therefore, by giving in that name ;
' and told him, the cruel ufage of my fchool-
' mafter, and the love I had for my companion,
' who I found was going away, had made me
' take this refolution ; and that I only requefted
' to be admitted as a failor's boy.

' The captain replied, ' Have a ftout heart,
' and you fhall be my boy ; but if you prove a
' coward, I will throw you over board."

" If

' If I do, ufe me as you pleafe; only give me
' leave, before you fail, to tell my father where
' I am; and that you have been fo good as to ac-
' cept of me.'

' He confented; and I wrote you word, fir,
' of my deftination; and affured you, whenever
' I had an opportunity, I would inform you
' where, and how I was; but this letter was
' not fent till the fhip was under fail, left you
' fhould prevent my fcheme taking place.

' The captain was very good to me; and had
' me inftructed in all the kind of learning, ne-
' ceffary for the profeffion I had chofen: and
' now all my Latin gave way to navigation, and
' the ftudy of the compafs.

' One dreadful night, when I was fo employ-
' ed, I heard a moft fhocking fcream; I ran up
' on deck, to enquire the caufe; the cry, from
' every mouth, was for mercy, and that we
' were loft!

' Whether

' Whether the fhip, that inftant, fplit, or
' what happened, I know not, for all was, from
' that moment, loft to me.

' My firft knowledge, after this fad period,
' was the finding myfelf in a hammock, amongft
' people I did not know ; who fpoke a language
' I could not underftand.

' I was fo weak, I could not move; an old
' man often fed me with a tea-fpoon. I per-
' ceived I was very ill; I was able, however,
' to count the days; and on the fifth day from
' the time my fenfes returned, the old man took
' me up, and carefully dreffed me ; and I was
' rejoiced to find, I had my watch, and my
' money that was in the clothes I had on, when
' I recollected going upon the deck of the Vic-
' tory.   I offered the good old man my money;
' he fmiling, ftroaked my head, but rejected
' the money; and gave me two blue fhirts ; and
' was thoroughly kind to me.

' I grew foon well, and as far as I could un-
' derftand, did every thing I thought they bid
                                        ' me

' me do.   I believe there were forty-five men in
' the veffel, befides myfelf.

' At the end of forty days, the fhip feemed
' ftrangely toffed about, and in every face, I
' read horror and defpair; and I fufpected, they
' did not know where they were.

' This lafted four days, the mifery plainly
' increafing—food grew fcarce; each day added-
' to that misfortune; and, in a fortnight's time,
' twenty men died.

' My grief was exceffive, at feeing my good
' old man failing: I had, for feveral days, given
' him two parts of the provifion that was allotted
' to me; he, finding himfelf going, gave me a
' bottle, and by figns, bid me take but little of
' it at a time.

' He foon after expired, which grieved me
' exceedingly; and I felt as if I had loft my only
' friend: indeed, though we could not make
' each

‘ each other underſtand what we ſaid, I had ex-
‘ perienced much kindneſs from his compaſſionate
‘ care of me.   I could not forbear letting the
‘ few ſurvivors ſhare my bottle, whilſt it laſted ;
‘ ſo it was ſoon exhauſted.

‘ At length, there was but one man and my-
‘ ſelf left alive : we were nearly ſtarved ; and
‘ that unhappy man died juſt before the ſhip ran
‘ a-ground, for want of hands to ſteer it.

‘ When the ſhip ſplit, a place diſcovered it-
‘ ſelf, which I (and probably many more in the
‘ veſſel) did not know of ; where there were a
‘ few poultry, and a little corn.   Had this been
‘ found ſooner, it might probably have ſaved
‘ a few lives.

‘ In my forlorn and helpleſs ſituation, it was
‘ of no uſe to me, and I gave myſelf up ; when,
‘ by the kindneſs of ſome men, in a kind of boat,
‘ I was almoſt miraculouſly ſaved.   Thus was I,

‘ in

' in the fpace of a few months (I know not how
' many !) twice refcued from the jaws-of death!

    ' Forgive this long detail—I fhould have ftopp-
' ed fooner; but obferving a kind attention,
' which could only proceed from the intereft
' taken in my prefervation; I could not refift
' the inclination I felt to continue my ftory,
' till I was in a fafe harbour;—A heart, now
' lightened from fo many forrows, as long op-
' preffed mine, gives a rapid utterance to a
' tongue, unufed to be very loquacious.'

My Lord faid, he fancied all his auditors, as
well as himfelf, had been too much entertained,
and too deeply interefted in his account, to think
he had been tedious; and he was certain, all
wifhed him to proceed to farther particulars of
a conduct, that had reflected honor on all be-
longing to him; but as he fhould be forry to tire
Mr. Mandeville, they would defer afking him
any of the many queftions, each muft long to
have anfwered.——Then rifing, told Colonel
                            Mandeville,

Mandeville, he muſt beg to ſpeak with him in his ſtudy ; and I heard his lordſhip ſay, as he paſſed me, ' It is time to conſult about the ' melancholy buſineſs we are to appear upon ſo ' ſoon.'—The horrid trial which is to be in a few days !

The recollection this has brought to my mind, makes me unfit, for the preſent, to write any more.

Indeed, I have already ſcribbled a moſt volu-minous packet ; but your wiſh to hear every par-ticular relating to this wonderful man, muſt plead my excuſe. As time permits, and occur-rences ariſe, I will add to my hiſtory. Adieu !

ANNE WILMOTT.

To

THE fates have decreed, that I ſhall be your correſpondent, by ſtopping the pen of your friend.—Now, perhaps you will fancy it is the praiſes you beſtow on my narratives, that makes me willing to continue them ; but you are miſtaken ;—my fondneſs for praiſe, is not extinguiſhed, for I am alive, and a woman ! but it pleaſes now, only from one mouth—there was a time, any mouth that uttered it, was certain of delighting me.

I expect you will confeſs I am very good, when thus engroſſed by one object, to find time to write to you ; however, to check your vanity, I muſt tell you, I do not devote thoſe hours to you, I could ſpend with that one ; but I am an

early

early rifer, and a late fitter up; I write faft, and am never idle; therefore I have more power of indulging the curiofity of my friends, than moft would have in my fituation.

Emily's pen is not laid by from idlenefs; but in playing with that fweet child (who hardly ever leaves her) fhe contrived to ftrain her right thumb, fo muft employ a deputy for fome time.

Her laft, fhe tells me, gave you an account of Mr. Mandeville's ftory, as far as we have heard it. I doubt not, but it was a very accurate repetition; for fhe liftened with attentive ears to each fyllable he fpoke; and her heart, I dare fay, vibrated to each account of 'dangers he had pafs'd!'

Read Othello's defcription of Defdemona's liftening to his tale of wonders, and it will give you a perfect idea of poor Emily——and fave me. me much trouble.

Yefterday morning, as fhe and I were chatting before breakfaft in the gallery, the child came

out

out of her father's dreffing-room, and ran up to us, and taking hold of my apron, faid, ' Pay ' come, and fee mama and Mifs Hoad.'

Not being able to guefs what fhe could mean, we let her guide us into the room, where we found Mr. Mandeville reading ; and two figures on the table, that almoft petrified me with af-tonifhment, from the very ftrong refemblance they had to Emily.—They were done in the fame manner of that we had feen at Meadow Houfe, refembling Mr. Mandeville.

He rofe, and throwing afide his book, faid, ' I am obliged to my little girl, I find, for the ' honor of feeing you here.—Dear creature, fhe ' will have it, thefe miniature ftatues are her ' mama, and Mifs Howard, I confefs, I too, fee ' the likenefs.'

Emily coloured ; and I laughing faid, ' They ' are her very felf ; but how is it poffible you ' could fo foon complete two fuch figures ? they ' are both alike, but I think you have flattered ' her.'

' Blefs

' Blefs me, Lady Anne, you furely do not
' ferioufly think me capable of taking a lady's
' likenefs, without her leave ; but truly, thefe
' figures do not fo ftrongly refemble Mifs How-
' ard, as fhe does my angel-like wife !'

Emily. faid, ' They were done for fifters, I
' fuppofe.'

' No,' faid the little prattler, ' mama, and
' Mifs Howard.'

' I cannot get that idea out of the child's head,
' which proves the likenefs ; but they were both
' done for my dear departed faint, in the drefs
' of the country ;—that, with the white feathers,
' reprefents the maiden daughter of an honor-
' able, with five ftones in the feathers ;—the
' black feathers, with feven ftones, is worn only
' by the wives of the honorables.'

I was much charmed with thefe beautiful images, and will try to defcribe them to you.

_ They are about twelve inches high, elegantly
dreffed, and with fweet countenances ; only that
                                                with

with the white feathers, feems to have a younger face than the other ; and has the moſt engagingly modeſt look you can conceive :—the other feems to be a little older, and to have, added to that modeſt innocent look, an air of dignity, but wholly from haughtineſs.

The dreſs of both, is a blue ſilk jacket, and petticoat ; with ſhort ſleeves, which reach only to the elbow, and is there turned up with white cambrick (or what appears ſo) pinked in a pattern, like lace ; a tucker the ſame.

The eldeſt figure had a white gauze, faſtened at the top of the left ſhoulder with diamonds, and hanging down to the right hip, where it was plaited cloſe with more diamonds ; and from thence, it flowed gracefully, ſo as to touch the ground ; and, as Mr. Mandeville told us, is occaſionally thrown over the head as a veil.

On the head of this figure, over ſhort, curling, light brown hair, was a ſmall white cap ; on the right ſide of which, there was a bunch of black feathers.

feathers, which hung from the head; and were tyed with a blue riband, that reached the other fide of the head, where it was faftened in bows; —amongft thefe feathers, were placed feven large diamonds.

In the younger figure, the veil was of filver gauze (fuch as this pretty child wears) the feathers were white; there was no cap; and inftead of diamonds, there were five amethyfts, mixed with the feathers, and amethyfts alfo to faften the veil on the hip and fhoulder, where the elder figure had diamonds; all the other parts of the drefs alike.

I faid, ' I never faw any thing fo beautiful, ' or fo pleafing, as thefe two figures.'

He replied, ' he had feen two as good; one for ever loft ! the other then prefent.'

Emily gave him a look, mingled with pleafure and confufion; then faid, with a blufhing check ' fhe feared Lady Belmont was waiting breakfaft,'

and

and so it proved; for our excuse I told her the cause of our rudeness.

Her ladyship requested to be indulged with a sight of the images.

Mr. Mandeville immediately went for them, and her ladyship saw the resemblance as strongly as I had done.

She enquired how the child came to call one of them mama, and not the other; she should have supposed she would naturally take them both for Miss Howard, as she concluded she could not recollect Mrs. Mandeville.

‘ I should imagine, madam, it is not possible
‘ she should; but I have before shewn her, that
‘ she calls her mama; and told her who it was
‘ for. The other she never saw, till to day, when
‘ I took it out of the box, to examine it parti-
‘ cularly.’

He left us to guess why!

That

That afternoon we miffed Mr. Mandeville, juft as we were going to tea, and could learn nothing more of him, than that, on hearing his child cry, ' he had gone haftily into the garden, ' to fee what ailed her.'

We all immediately went thither, to look for him ; but foon flackened our paces, on hearing the fweeteft pipe that ever charmed my ear.

Accuftomed as I have been in Italy, to the moft melodious voices, I felt, in every nerve, that I had never before liftened to fuch founds.

I could almoft hate this man for excelling in fo many ways, not only the generality of his fex, but even my beloved Harry, his unfortunate brother.

I turned to Belville, affuring him that I fhould certainly leave him to wear the willow, if I were convinced I could prevail on Mr. Mandeville to return my paffion.

The

The confident wretch, with a ſmile, ſaid,
‘ Then I am pretty ſecure, ſor Mr. Mandeville
‘ has declared, there can be no virtue, which is
‘ not founded upon juſtice.’

When we came up to the ſeat, and mentioned how we had been delighted, Mr. Mandeville told us, that finding his little darling had
got a fall, he had began ſinging a little favorite
ſong of her’s, to divert her attention from the
pain her tumbling had given her ; and inadver-
tently had gone on, and ſung a ſong of more
compaſs, when the child had left him to go to
her maid, for a longer walk.

Lady Belmont entering the octagon temple,
which ſhe had not done for ſeveral months, ſaid,

‘ As the afternoon is ſo fine, ſuppoſe we drink
‘ our tea here; and, perhaps Mr. Mandeville
‘ will be ſo kind as to purſue the hiſtory he began
‘ yeſterday.

‘ With gratitude to heaven, I own your re-
‘ turn has proved a peculiar bleſſing ! in allevi-
‘ ating

' ating forrows I thought nothing could have
' leffened.'

She wiped her eyes, and after a figh, faid—

' I think you much the fame in face, you was
' in your childhood; when you was always a
' great favorite with me.

' I ever thought you very like your poor mo-
' ther—a very excellent woman !

' She was as partially fond of you, as your
' father was fuppofed to be of your brother.—
' Do you remember her at all !'

' Yes, madam, but not fo perfectly as I did
' your ladyfhip; I never have forgotten that,
' the laft time I was at home, before I left
' fchool, your ladyfhip heard me read, and
' gave me a guinea, and a very pretty pocket
' book, faying,—Charles, be a good boy, and
' I will love you for your mother's fake.'

' I re-

"I recollect it," said Lady Belmont, and hear-
' tily have I wept for the sad fate we suppofed
' had befallen you; and thought it a comfort
' your poor mother had not lived to fee that
' day :—but the decrees of providence are above
' our comprehenfion!

' We grieve for thofe, who, if acquainted
' with our fenfations, pity our folly.'

Poor Lady Belmont's pity had pierced her own
heart!—her voice faultered, and fhe could not
proceed.

Mr. Mandeville perceiving her diftrefsful feelings, immediately turned the fubject, juft as
my Lord and the Colonel joined us, by faying,
rather abruptly—

' Your ladyfhip afked, yefterday, if my wife
' was fair : I do not recollect that I anfwered
' you then (as I truly could) that fhe was fair,
' was wife, and as good as human nature could
' be !

' The

' The natives of Youngland are all white;
' that circumftance, and the name of their
' country, confirm my idea, that they came
' originally from England.

'. They have a natural benevolence; I was
' treated with an humanity that would have done
' honor to chriftians, even before I was of any
' age; and when, of courfe, I was looked upon
' as the loweft perfon in the kingdom.'

' Why,' faid the Colonel, ' fhould they de-
' fpife you fo much? you was an acute fenfible
' lad at fchool; furely they did not take you for
' an ideot.'

' No, fir, but we muft allow for national cuf-
' toms; age is with them honorable; but no
' one can attain it, in their country, let them
' live ever fo many fprings, till they have, by
' fome means or other, proved beneficial to the
' country, fo that a perfon may become honor-
' able; that is to fay, may be fixty years of age
' when he is very young; and he may have lived
' fixty

' fixty fprings, and ftill be deemed of no age :
' or he may, by mifconduct, go back to ten
' year s of age, from fixty.

' Had I chofen to have continued in Young-
' land, I fhould immediately have been feventy;
' when I married I was fixty.'

A general laugh enfued—the firft that has been
heard in thefe gardens, fince the unhappy walk
I took with Lady Julia !

My Lord afked Emily, if fhe could like to live
in a country, where the older a man was, the
more defirable for a hufband ?

She replied, fhe had always refpected age,
when only acquired by living long ; but when
it arofe from growing old in virtue, it muft furely
be ftill more eftimable.

Mr. Mandeville's eyes brightened with pleafure, at the artlefs manner in which fhe difplay-
ed fentiments fo favourable to him.

I hoped

I hoped fecretly that his lordfhip would fee how matters were, and was fufficiently cured of experiments, to be content to let this couple proceed in the beaten path. Alas! he has dearly paid for the winding one he planned before!

We had more chat, but I have not more time at prefent, fo muft haften to fay, adieu.

ANNE WILMOTT.

To

To Mr. HERBERT.

I CANNOT pretend to write methodically—method was never my forte; and now, it would be very unreaſonable indeed, to expect I ſhould try for it.

I think, therefore, you will be content with my penning down ſuch converſations, as I imagine you would have been pleaſed to be preſent at.

But before I relate any, I muſt tell you, that Lady Belmont's ſpirits are ſo much exhilarated by the late fortunate events, that I flatter myſelf, when you return to this part of the world, ſhe will be able to enjoy your company; and I am ſure your compaſſion has made you forgive her ladyſhip's having hitherto ſhunned it.

Perſons

Perfons who have been fo feverely wounded, do not difcriminate, nicely, the caufe of their fuffering: could fhe have done this, fhe muft have feen that her's had been owing to poor Harry's impetuofity, more than to your unfortunate forgetfulnefs, in not leaving his addrefs with your fervant.

My Lord's ftronger mind, enabled him to diftinguifh more juftly.

Pity her, therefore, but do not condemn her; for fhe has an amiable as well as a fufceptible heart!

Now to my ftory—

Colonel Mandeville afked his fon, the other afternoon, from whence he concluded the country and religion of thefe Indians, had formerly been the fame as ours.

G                                    ' I believe,

' I believe, fir, I mentioned to you the great
' fimilitude in the language to ours ; though they
' knew nothing of the art of writing, till I was
' happy enough to inftruct them in it ; and had
' only four books, which neither they nor I
' could read.

' As any thing ftruck me particularly, I wrote
' it down ; and when we could converfe, enquir-
' ed into the meaning of what I had not under-
' ftood ; and wrote down all the inftructions I
' received, which proved a great help to me.

' I foon found they worfhipped one fupreme
' Being ; whom they believed to be the God of
' heaven and earth.

' They could repeat the creed, the Lord's
' prayer, and the ten commandments—faid they
' were taught from generation to generation,
' that they were to learn thefe ; and not to make
' any alteration in their religion, till a man or
' men, fhould come amongft them, dreffed as a
                                        ' painting

' painting defcribed, and fhould inftruct them
' out of a book he would call the bible.

' This painting I faw, when I attained the
' age of ten years, in their eftimation ; and I
' found it be a picture of an Englifh clergyman,
' dreffed exactly as ours are.

' Their church ftands in a large piece of
' ground, about fix acres ; which is walled
' round : a row of very large trees furrounds it.

' There are doors out of this wall, which
' open into fquare rooms, about ten feet high ;
' which are repofitories for whatever they think
' worth preferving, and tranfmitting to pofte-
' rity ; which they do by paintings, as well as
' we do by writing ; or at leaft, fo as to be very
' intelligible.

' In one of thefe rooms, the original fettle-
' ment is delineated ; there are four pair of men
' and women, hand in hand ; preceded by one
G 2                    ' man,

' man, who ſtands by himſelf, holding a croſs
' in his hand.

' The firſt couple is followed by ſeven chil-
' dren; the ſecond by ſix; the third by five;
' and the laſt by two, only.

' In the next room, is a melancholy repreſen-
' tation of the man with the croſs, expiring;
' many of the men and women lying dead, and
' all the children, excepting eight.

' In the next room, is a painting of the few
' ſurvivors; amongſt which, I reckoned eight
' children; the eldeſt ſeemed to be under nine
' years old, and was a girl; and there was one
' child not three years old.

' They have a tradition, that no one, who
' was above twelve years old when they went
' thither, ever ſurvived two years.

' From

' From thefe eight children, defcended all
' the prefent race of Younglanders; for they
' only are white, the neighbouring nations are
' tawny.

' In the next room, is painted the Lord's
' prayer, creed, and ten commandments.

' In the next, rules (which are as laws to
' them; and more ftrictly obferved, than our
' laws are amongft us.)

' Some of thefe rules are, that a man muft
' be twenty years before he is a fire; fires, are
' under the direction of ancients, who are al-
' ways above that age; ancients are directed
' by honorables, who are fixty; and honorables,
' are under the command of the moft honorable;
' who is chofen by the unanimous voices of
' each clafs or tribe, of fires, ancients, and ho-
' norables.—When chofen, he is deemed fe-
' venty.

' I conclude

' I conclude you bear in mind, I am not
' talking of the number of springs they have feen,
' but of the age allotted to them, according to
' their conduct.

' The moft honorable is never more than one
' perfon at a time : he can lay down his dignity,
' if he has the confent of the tribes, but not
' otherwife ; and they can degrade him, if he
' fhould turn out unworthy of the great poft he
' has acquired ; but then it muft be done by
' the unanimous voice of each clafs, or tribe.

' Every tribe is diftinguifhed by their cc.ours ;
' the fires are white, the ancients green, the ho-
' norables blue, and the moft honorable red.

' Every perfon, male or female, muft wear
' the colour of the tribe to which they belong.

' The heads of that tribe, wear filks ; the in-
' feriors ftuffs :—nothing is left for fancy, but
' the ornaments on the head and ftomachers
                                          ' of

‘ of the fair fex; which they may adorn as their
‘ tafte directs, only diftinguifhing their tribe
‘ by their colour; and their rank in it, by fea-
‘ thers in their head; and the degrees of that
‘ rank, by the number and kind of precious
‘ ftones, mixed with thofe feathers.

‘ The fingle women cannot wear diamonds,
‘ or more than five ftones, though daughters of
‘ an honorable: the wives muft wear a kind of
‘ cap; if wives of an honorable, they muft wear
‘ black feathers, and have feven diamonds mix-
‘ ed with them..

‘ All who have not arrived to the clafs of fires,
‘ eat promifcuoufly with the dependents (or fer-
‘ vants, as we fhould call them) in a lower hall.

‘ The fires, ancients, and honorables, eat in
‘ an upper hall; but the food is exactly the fame
‘ in both—wholefome, clean, and well (though
‘ plainly) dreffed :—no luxuries of any kind.

                                        ‘ An

' An infant is brought by its parents to church ;
' where it is, by a painting, regiſtered in the
' tribe in which it is born; and an hymn ſung
' ſuitable to the occaſion, which very ſimply ex-
' preſſes, a thankſgiving for the birth of a child ;
' and a hope, if it is a boy, it will deſerve to be
' moſt honorable ; if a girl, that it may be the
' mother of a moſt honorable ; the Lord's pray-
' er, creed, and ten commandments, are then
' repeated, which cloſes their ceremony of bap-
' tiſm.

' When a couple is to be married, the bride
' is led to church, by her father, or neareſt of
' kin ; an honorable meets them at the entrance,
' with a gold chain, and a lock at one end of it.
' This chain he puts over them both, then locks
' it, and throws the key into a pit, which runs
' into the river ; a hymn is then ſung, expreſ-
' ſive of their wiſhes, that they may live happily,
' and produce a race of honorables, or mothers
' of honorables ; then. the Lord's prayer, &c.
' are repeated, as at baptiſm.

' The

' The married couple go home, attended by
' all the friends of each ; the chain is then taken
' off,  by flipping it over their heads ;  and care-
' fully laid by,  as their moft valuable poffeffion.

' They have a piece of ground allotted to each
' tribe for a burying-place ;  that for the moft
' honorables,  is,  of courfe,  the fmalleft.

' I fhould have mentioned,  that amongft the
' repofitories,  there is a room,  filled  with all
' the neceffary wearables for children ;  and all
' the articles for their immediate or future ufe ;
' which is conftantly to be kept full, as it is from
' the common ftock ;  every child is to be fuppli-
' ed,  till it is paft ten years of age.

' They have  one law (or rule, as they call
' them) which is, that any man, having lived
' twenty-five fprings,  without gaining any age,
' is then to become a member of fome ufeful oc-
' cupation for the good of the whole community ;
' but if they invent any new art, or become par-

G 3                              ' ticularly

' cularly famous in thofe already known, they
' gain the age of ten years, and fo may advance
' in years according to their merit.

' This clafs is diftinguifhed by wearing yel-
' low; and they may marry whilft in it; but
' their wives muft go into their clafs, and wear
' their colour, till an advance in age, entitles
' them to a higher diftinction.

' The rule that appeared to me the moft un-
' reafonable, is, that if a woman, by accident,
' or choice, fleeps one night, in any man's
' houfe, without one of her parents, or next of
' kin being with her, in the fame houfe; the
' mafter of the houfe, or his fon, if either are
' fingle, may, after daylight, demand her in
' marriage, if they choofe it.

' She has the liberty of refufing, but it is upon
' hard conditions; becaufe fhe muft then leave
' her father's houfe in a fortnight's time, and

go

' go into the clafs of ufeful employments; any
' one of which fhe may choofe that beft fuits
' her tafte and abilities; and in that clafs fhe
' muft continue, and wear its colour; unlefs
' marrying into a higher tribe (which there is no
' rule againft) gives her a right to become one
' of them, and to wear their colour of courfe.'

' I think I muft have fatigued my audience,
' I am fure I have myfelf; but I hope, fir,' turning to his father, ' you fee reafons now to be of
' my opinion, that thefe Indians came originally
' from England.'

The Colonel acknowledged he did; and wifhed
their mother country had made as wife laws for
themfelves, as had been made by their colony.

Before we went to bed, my Lord called me
into his ftudy, and told me, he thought the papers Mr. Ware had given him, fhould now be
perufed by us all; as they would make us all
acquainted

acquainted with Mr. Mandeville's conduct, and character; and elucidate many particulars in his narration; but as they muſt be painful to Mr. Mandeville to hear, for many reaſons, he begged an opportunity might be taken in his ab-ſence, to peruſe them.

He ſaid, we had beſt copy them amongſt us; for he deſired the originals ſhould be returned to him; as he meaned to preſerve them with great care, that they might deſcend to future generations.

As my pen and fingers are equally worn out, I have deſired Colonel Belville to employ his leiſure hours in tranſcribing them; by which contrivance, I ſhall abridge him of many op-portunities of teazing me to fix an important criſis of my fate, which I am coward enough to dread;——and ſhall relieve myſelf more ways than one.

When

When he has written enough to make a packet you fhall receive it from,

Your's, &c.

ANNE WILMOTT.

MEMOIRS

# M E M O I R S

## Written by Mrs. MANDEVILLE,

*And given into Mr. Ware's hands, a little before her death.*

W H E N the dear giver of every home-felt joy to me, fhall happily arrive (as I pray to God he may) in his native land, the innate goodnefs of his heart will, I am convinced, drefs my character to his friends, in the dignity of his own virtues; when, alas, how few would have fallen to my fhare, but for him!

He found my mind like an uncultivated piece of land: no pains had been taken, but to prevent

vent noifome weeds, from choaking its original
virtue ; for all nature has fome, even in infancy,
if clofely attended to, we may difcover a tenden-
cy to right or wrong principles.

The improving the former, and eradicating
the latter, as they happen to appear, fhould be
the governing defign of every inftructor.

My parents took every poffible care to keep
my mind from error, by permitting me to fee
only what was good, and keeping from my knowledge every thing that could degrade human nature.

I was their only child, and had lived eight
fprings, when my mother, by a fall, broke her
leg.

It was attended by no worfe confequences,
than the unavoidable pain and confinement ; during which time I had never left her, but ftrove,

by

by all the little attentions my juvenile years could pay, to leſſen her uneaſineſs.

My father had, as well as herſelf, obſerved my aſſiduity with pleaſure; and one fine after-noon my father ſaid to me,

'Agnes, your dutiful care of your mother
'has given me great ſatisfaction; but I think
'ſuch conſtant attention, and confinement, may
'hurt your health: I perceive you neither eat,
'or look ſo well, as you did before this accident;
'therefore, you ſhall ride with me to day; and
'to reward you for being ſo good a girl, I will
'ſhew you a new ſight; and the exerciſe and
'air, may give you a better reliſh for your ſup-
'per.'

My mother ſaid, 'Go, my dear, I am quite
'eaſy this afternoon.'

Without any inducement of amuſement, I had been taught that obedience was the moſt neceſſary

duty

duty of a child, and the foundation of all other merits.

I flew, therefore, to prepare for my little excursion; and soon saw my little horse at the door, with my father's.

Observe, though I call it a horse, yet I now know, we have no horses in Youngland; but we call every creature by that name on which we ride; sometimes it is an afs, a calf, a large dog, a deer, &c.

As we rode, we met my two coufins, Hubert and Mirza.

My father afked them, if they would accompany us; adding,

' I am going to fhew Agnes the fea, which,
' as it is quite new to her, I expect it will delight
' and pleafe her much.'

We

We all clambered up the sides of very steep mountains, covered with woods; and much higher than I had ever mounted before.

We then quitted our horses, and walked on a delightful plain; bounded on three sides by the sea, the setting sun illumined every object.

My father observed, with every mark of plea-sure, the rapturous astonishment, which appear-ed in my face; and felt all a parent's delight at my remarks; answering my questions in a man-ner that, ' made my senses tutors to my mind.'

As I went very near the brow of a rock, which hung over the sea, he called out to me to be care-ful; and asked what I looked at so attentively? I said, ' on yonder great moving thing; is it a ' fish?'

He came to the part I stood on; and when I had pointed it out to him, said, ' no! child, I
' think

' think it is not a fish; but I will soon know
' certainly, then calling to my cousins, he
' said.'

' Hubert, do you see Agnes safe home, and
' your brother and I will try to find out what that
' is, we see yonder.'

So saying, he and Mirza struck rapidly into a
wood, hanging on one side of the mountain;
and Hubert and I returned home.

In about two hours afterwards, arrived my father, accompanied by three men, who had several baskets in their hands; but my father
brought the precious burthen, which was a boy,
seemingly dead.

He carried him to his own bed, giving the
men some orders about the things they had
brought.

My

My father continued, till long after I was in bed, with this boy.

The next morning at breakfast, he said to me.

' Agnes, I promifed to tell you what that was, ' you fhowed me on the fea——I then faw it ' was part of a veffel, in diftrefs ; fo took Mirza ' a fhort way I knew through the woody fide of ' the mountain, down to the water fide ; from ' whence I got boats, and took men, ropes, and ' every thing we could collect in a fhort time ; ' and went to the fpot you pointed to, where we ' difcovered a melancholy fight indeed ; part of ' a fhip, in which were found dead men (one ' hardly cold) and one boy who feemed expi- ' ring; fome half ftarved fowls and various ar- ' ticles.

' All that had any figns of life left, we brought ' away ;

' away; and left people to take care of such
' things as could be saved.'

My mother said, she feared the poor child
could not live; he was too weak to speak, and
could hardly open his eyes.

' My father replied, ' he was doubtless very
' near dead; and, though I never saw the me-
' dicines we have given him, have so little ef-
' fect, in such a number of hours, yet, I am
' not without hopes, as he is undoubtedly bet-
' ter than when I found him.

' I conclude the ship he was in, has by some
' storms, been driven out of its course; and pro-
' bably has been tossed about long enough, to
' have the poor creatures that were in it, starv-
' ed to death;——the four corps we saw, had
' that appearance.

' We will do our best for this unfortunate
' child;

' child; the event is in the hands of God: I
' have sent for the most skilful man I know, to
' direct what is fittest for his case.

' If he lives, he may reward our cares; if he
' dies, the consciousnefs, that we have done our
' duty by him, will be a reward.'

Three days passed, before there were any hopes
of his life; on the fourth he gave some signs of
returning senfes.

In this time, I had twice seen him, and I
cried heartily, at so sad a fight.

My mother commended me for feeling so much
compaffion; and with her eyes full of tears
faid.

' I grieve for his poor parents, who are pro-
' bably, now lamenting the lofs of him.'

She

She fent me, however, to divert me, to feed the poultry; tho'e that were brought from the fhip, I fed firft, becaufe they were ftrangers; and gave them a fecond feeding, as they were moft hungry.

One amongft thefe, I thought prettier than the reft; and when I returned, afked, ' If that ' might not be mine?'

My father looked at me with more fternnefs than I had ever feen in his face before; and faid,

' Girl, do you confider what you afk? is it ' mine to give.'

' Why not father, you took them from no ' body; but for you they muft all have died; ' and would die now, if you did not feed ' them.'

' True

' True, Agnes ; yet, who do you think has
' the beft right to them, the poor fick boy, or,
' I ?'


' The boy.' ' Certainly,' faid my father;
' you would think fo if you were in his place ;
' and never forget, what I told you once be-
' fore, that you are always to do by others,
' what you would have others do by you ;
' and then, you will never be unjuft ; for
' nobody choofes to  have others unjuft to
' them.'


' Oh, then I know why you are fo kind to
' this poor boy ; becaufe, if I was from home,
' ftarved and almoft dead, you would wifh fuch
' care fhould be taken of me, as you now take
' of him.'


My father melted into tears, kiffed me, and
faid, ' yes ! my dear girl.'

' Then

‘ Then I will feed his fowls carefully, and
‘ they shall be all his if he lives.’

The fifth day, the doctor said, he had never known the remedies he had applied, of so little use ; he believed, indeed, his senses were returned, though he spoke but seldom ; and then,
what could not be underftood ; but that he had
shewn a wonderful aptness to learn—his situation
confidered—for in about an hour after he heard
somebody say father, he had repeated the word
very right ; and then added several more, which
nobody present could underftand.

The doctor then told my father, his longer
stay could be of no use—that he had given him
the laft medicine in his power to adminifter—
that if this cordial did not revive him, he would
die by the next rifing of the sun ; if he outlived
that hour, he would probably recover.

My father said, then he would fit and watch
him, till that time was paft.

H

He did fo, and the poor boy flept fix hours
——waked refreshed——eat fome of fuch food
as the doctor had ordered to be given to him,
and went to fleep again.

The fun being now quite rifen, and the boy
apparently mending, my father went to lie down
for fome hours.

After he got fome fleep, he rofe, and went to
the poor boy's room; and in a few minutes came
to my mother, and faid, he believed he had
faved the life of a very good child; becaufe, when
he opened the door, he heard a weak voice pro-
nouncing what he could not underftand; and
as he went farther into the room, he faw the poor
creature on his knees, by the bed fide, and fo
intent on the duty he was performing, that he did
not take any notice of him.

So he withdrew to the door, without fpeaking
to difturb him, at his prayers, for fo, he verily
believed, he was employed; for though he could

not

not underſtand all he ſaid, yet he diſtinctly heard the words, God and Father, pronounced ſeveral times.

He ſaid the poor boy was weeping heartily.

From this time, he recovered ſurpriſingly faſt; and ſpoke very often for a great while together, what we could not underſtand; yet he ſoon knew many of our words.

The method in which he expreſſed his thanks, was by bowing, which he would often do; and I thought in a much prettier manner, than any body I had ever ſeen.

He would alſo often kiſs my father's hand; and I uſed to wonder, he never kiſſed mine.

On the eighth day, he was able to riſe early, and put on his clothes himſelf.

The next day he was able to come out of his

H 2                                              room;

room; and on the following Sunday, hearing fomebody fay the word church, he immediately repeated the word, held up his hands, and turning about, kneeled down, with his face to the wall.

My father thought he would like to go to church, and join in our devotion; and fo afked him, by figns and words; he underftood enough of both to fhew he wifhed to do fo; and accordingly went with us; but, as he has fince told us, was much furprized to find our church, and form of worfhip, fo different from what he expected.

To our equal furprize, he repeated the Lord's prayer, &c. as well as we could ourfelves; yet he could not fay any of the hymns; excepting the word God, and a few other words.

A month paffed on, without any extraordinary event.

He

He learned our language ; and whilft he was acquiring it, we, almoft imperceptibly, learned his.

My father was very kind to him, and very fond of him ; yet he never let him eat at our table.

One day, I afked if Charles Woodville might not dine with us.

' No,' replied my father ; ' when he has ' gained any age, he fhall be treated accord- ' ingly ; but in the mean time, why fhould he ' be treated differently from our own natives ?

' Till he is ten years of age, you know he ' cannot have a home of his own, let the num- ' ber of his fprings be what they will.'

' Poor child,' faid my mother, he will never ' have one ; for no foreigner ever lived two ' fprings here.'

I hope

I hope otherwife,' faid my father; I have fo
' great an affection for him, that I have had a
' confultation between his doctor, and the moft
' experienced perfons amongft us.

' It appears that his conftitution is a particular
' one; for when fo near dying, he did not feem
' to have any complaint but weaknefs; and of
' that, with all others, the high cordials he took,
' generally perfected a cure in twelve hours;
' with him, it was feveral days, before they took
' any effect.

' Then again, I have hopes from his age;
' for our paintings fhew us, that all under twelve
' fprings lived, and I do not think he reckons
' more.'

My father's hopes were verified:—the dear
Woodville—for dear he was then to me, though
my young heart was unconfcious of its feeling
more than pity for him—grew in ftrength and
beauty, to every body's admiration.

He

He never ſtaid longer in the eating-hall, than the meal made neceſſary; yet behaved when there, with ſuch cheerfulneſs and good-nature, that all his companions in it loved him.

He was ever employed in ſome kind. of ſtudy; and in two months, was as perfect in our lan-guage, as if he had been a native.

My father often was with him, in his retired hours; and he ſelected a ſet of young people, whom he aſſociated together, and called it, ' A youthful ſociety for uſeful arts.'

Each was to endeavour to find out ſome new one, or improve upon thoſe already known.

Woodville produced writing upon paper; till then, painting was the only method of delinea-ting their thoughts to a perſon at a diſtance, or of tranſmitting them to poſterity.

The utility of this new method, was mentioned

ned to the heads of feveral tribes; and Woodville expatiated fo clearly upon its advantages, that they were all charmed with the difcovery; and the honorables petitioned the moft honorable to confer a reward upon Woodville.

'The moft honorable, whofe greateft pleafure it is to reward merit, fent for him the next day, and afked him which tribe he chofe, to be enrolled in.

Giving him a painted table, and bid him give it to the head of that tribe he chofe; explaining to him the nature of this enrollment; then fhook him by the hand, with great cordiality; and told him, he hoped, as he found their nation was fo prone to reward merit, it would infpire him with the noble ambition of deferving the continuance of favors from that country, which had now put him upon the fame footing, as any native, who was made ten years of age; which is always the firft period given to any.

Our

Our people know not what the word politenefs means, but exprefs their fentiments in a plain, unaffected, and generally, very concife manner; but they all proved, that they had no diflike to more polifhed language; for they were all charm-ed with the refpectful, modeft, and yet dignified manner, with which this young man received their favors.

When he came home, how lovely did he ap-pear; his face was brightened with an unufual cheerfulnefs—had a manly ferenity, yet had loft none of its natural modeft air.

My father, who had been witnefs of what had paffed at the affembly of the honorables, and moft honorable; for the firft time, took him by the hand; faying,

' Woodville, I wifh you joy of your early ad-
' vancement; I hope it is an earneft of future
' rewards to your merit.'

H3                         ' I fhall!

' I shall rejoice to see your age advance rapid-
' ly to seventy.'

He thanked my father, with his eyes filled with
grateful tears.

Then respectfully bowing, he put the painted
table into my father's hand; requesting him to
accept it.

My father looked it over, said,

' With real pleasure, I receive you into my
' tribe, and am glad it is your choice; some lit-
' tle forms are necessary, according to our rules—
' to-morrow you shall choose your abode, and be
' furnished out of the common stock.'

He modestly replied, ' My youth and igno-
' rance, will, I hope, plead my excuse, if I
' omit any of the proper tokens of respect, that
' can shew my gratitude to you; who, next to
' the Almighty, have been the preserver of my
' life;

' life ; and enabled me to make that life a blef-
' fing,  by fhewing me how to gain a reputation,
' which reflects more honor upon you,  than upon
' me.

' I can only fay,  I ftill beg your advice ; that
' my conduct may anfwer my wifhes, and make
' me  a worthy member of your tribe.'

From this day,  he was conftantly at our table,
and a ftill more conftant inhabitant of my heart ;
which trembled,  when  my  mother afked him
how many fprings he had lived.

I dared hardly allow  myfelf to breathe, whilft
he told her, that he fancied he was  not eleven ;
he knew he was but a little paft ten,  when he
left England, and he thought that could not be
twelve months ago.

The joy I felt, was inexpreffible, on hearing he
was not arrived at the fatal period.

He

He continued his studies in his own house, and in two springs compleated a book to prove, that we were originally of the same country; from the similitude of the name of England and Youngland; of many words in each language; of our worshipping the Deity, by the same appellation; and in some parts in the same form, as the Lord's prayer, creed, and ten commandments; but he should be better able to shew this, when the heads of his tribe gave him leave to go over the whole nation.

My father (who spent many hours every day with him, and, as well as myself, and many others, had been taught the art of writing by him) quickly replied,

‘ You will hardly gain my approbation for
‘ that scheme; because our people are bordered
‘ with neighbours of a very different disposition
‘ —tawny men, fierce in their natures, and cruel
‘ in their practices; destroying in a barbarous
                                    ‘ manner,

' manner, all who go to them, and are ftran-
' gers.'

He was therefore obliged to be content with
this anfwer; for two fprings more, we faw little
of him at our houfe; but my ears were daily delighted with his praifes.

' The wonderful young man,' as he was generally called, was the theme of every tongue:
fo early did he infpire every perfon, that the old
liftened with ferious attention; the young were
only happy in feeing and hearing him; and I,
far happier than any other, when fo bleft.

At the end of four fprings, he gained confent
to be abfent t o fprings; and to take with him
any five of his young companions who chofe to
go.

During which time, he was to fend a meffenger once a month, with a written account of his
employment.

By

By thefe, it was found, he diffufed knowledge wherever he went; and was a general benefactor.

But my father (who received the greateft delight from thefe teftimonies of Woodville's merit) was much furprized one morning, when he faw the moft honorable approach our dwelling, followed by fix men, each bearing a piece of painting.

This was a very unufual thing; for the moft honorable ufed to fend for thofe he wanted to fpeak with, and never hardly condefcended to go to them.

All the refpect our fimple manners permit was fhown.

My father went out to meet, and conduct him in; and my mother, and the reft of the family, were ranged on the outfide the door, to welcome him.

His

His greatnefs feated himfelf, and then faid,

‘ Friend, as you have been the preferver of
‘ the wonderful young man, enrolled into your
‘ tribe, it is fit to reward your care, by telling
‘ you, he proves a moft excellent member of the
‘ community.

‘ I have therefore myfelf conducted hither the
‘ meffengers from fix tribes (which you know is
‘ near half our nation) which have been fent
‘ with paintings of the great fervices he has per-
‘ formed amongft them.

‘ Order the bearers to open the paintings, and
‘ to give their own account.’

This being done, the moft honorable faid,

‘ The honorables have defired I would fhew
‘ my wonted juftice, in conferring favors on their
‘ great benefactor.

I have

'I have confidered the paintings, and liftened
' to the bearers accounts; and, as a reward to
' his deferts, I decree, that he fhall have a room
' in the wall of the church yard, devoted to thefe
' trophies of his merit, as our anceftors have
' had—you fhall keep the key.

' On the outfide of the door, paint his device,
' the fame that is put on his houfe door, and
' mark him aged forty.

' Ten years we gave him before he went out;
' I add five now, for each tribe he has fo well
' ferved :—adding, ' he is the firft youth, who
' has not feen fifteen fprings, that ever gained
' forty years.

' If he returns home with unfullied credit, I
' mean to meet him with a welcome that will
' pleafe him.'

One of the ftrangers replied,

' Alas !

' Alas ! he will come back to you ; wherever he has been, every method has been tried to prevail on him to continue there, but all in vain ; he fays, he muft go home (meaning here) and then, when he can quit home (meaning where he came from) to England, to a father who grieves for him.

' He will not accept of any authority with us, except to direct us, which is for our own benefit."

All the ftrangers faid the fame, and that ' He had taught many of them his language, and fome to write—we all endeavour to receive his inftruction—we fee in his looks he is as honeft, as we find him brave, generous and humane ; and our rules tell us, we are never to fufpect, before we have been deceived; nor ever again truft the man who has deceived us ; but this young, and virtuous man, will never deceive us.'

The

The moſt honorable replied,

'  I like your gratitude, and I hope you are ſa-
' tisfied with my juſtice.

'  Tell your heads, what I have done to prove
' both.

'  To Woodville, ſay—that he has deſervedly
' attained the age of forty—he has full liberty
' to go where he pleaſes, and to ſtay as long as
' he pleaſes ; as we rely on his truth and honor,
' that he will return to us, the Ten Tribes of
' Cantwell Plains, in Youngland.'

Alas, this meſſage damped the joy I had
felt.

I had counted the hours of his abſence, with
heart-felt tranſport——I ſaw the allotted time was
nearly expired.

But

But my time of forrow was to be lengthened--. he had leave to prolong his ftay ; and wellIknew where glory and honor called, he would conti· nue.

However, I determined to devote my time to the improvement of myfelf fo much, that I might make an impreffion on the only heart I wifhed to gain.

In this manner, three more fprings were fpent ; and then fome fad months, in which we neither faw, nor heard from him.

All were uneafy ; my parents greatly fo ; but their concern was but the anxiety of friendfhip— mine proceeded (though unknown to myfelf) from a tenderer fource.

My mifery was greatly increafed, by my fa· ther's talking to me of marriage—mentioned the youths who had chofen me ; and bid me fix on him I moft approved.

Alas,

Alas, he was not there! and were he come, how could I be sure he would prefer me?

I wept, and pleaded with my father.

Whether he guessed the true cause of my rejecting offers which fairer maids would have approved, I know not; but he yielded to my intreaties and dismissed lovers I could not accept.

At the end of seven springs and a half, from the time Woodville had left us, I saw my father return one morning, from the mansion of the most honorable; with such pleasure in his face, as made my heart tremble with joy, ere he spoke.

He soon confirmed my hopes, by saying, that -yesterday, messengers arrived at the mansion, with the welcome account, that six of their oldest chiefs were conducting Woodville home, with all marks of gratitude:——that they were to stop at Luton, three miles off.

- He

He called all his dependants, and gave them orders to fpend the day in feftivity; and lay afide all bufinefs, from eight in the morning till fun-fet; and the next day to prepare to meet the re-turning hero.

The next morning every thing was fo altered, one could hardly know either the place or the people.

All were adorned with things never brought out, but on great occafions; and every body feemed cloathed in diamonds and precious ftones.

Select bands of people playing on various kinds of mufic; others finging; others carrying the moft refrefhing, and pleafant liquors.

We have none that intoxicate—mirth and drunkennefs do not unite with us.

Others with bafkets of fweet-meats, and cakes; others with bafkets of flowers, to ftrew the way.

Each

Each party keeping clofe to each other, yet in great order, and all in the colour of our tribe, which was blue, ornamented varioufly, where we were allowed to difplay our fancy.

My hours, from the time of my father's arrival, had been devoted—may I own my weaknefs, to making my poor felf appear as amiable as I could.

Never had I taken fo much pains—never had I fo little fucceeded, in my own opinion.

So long had I altered and changed my ornaments, that my mother, who waited for me, grew impatient, and we reached the manfion but juft in time; for the moft honorable was fetting out, accompanied by the honorables, all in heir robes of dignity—then the ancients, and the fires—then the young men, according to their age—then the youths of no age—next

followed

followed the matrons—and laft, went the maid-
ens.

We walked flowly on, for about half an hour,
in this order ; when mufic began, on the fight of
the party we went to meet.

We foon perceived people bearing Woodville's
trophies ; that is to fay, paintings of the great
actions he had performed.

When the hero, and the ancients with him
appeared in fight, the trophy bearers parted of
each fide, as did our proceffion, and made a lane
for the chiefs and the hero.

They prefented him to the moft honorable.

The modeft, yet dignified appearance, his
beautiful perfon made on that interefting occafion, is as far beyond the powers of my defcrib-
ng, as the effects it had on my heart, are im-
poffible

poſſible to be underſtood by any, but thoſe who have loved like me!

He reſpectfully bowed to the moſt honorable firſt —gratefully receiving the favors conferred on him; then, generally to all; but with a marked diſtinction in his manner, to my parents; but of me, did not ſeem to take any particular notice; ough (as he has ſince told me) his heart felt all the animation, the ſight of a loved object, long abſent, muſt give to a feeling mind.

During this ceremony, the melody of voices, and harmony of the accompanying inſtruments, chaunting his praiſes, muſt have charmed every ear, that was not cloſed for ever.

The converſation was wholly on his exploits; it was remarkable, that the relators of them, ſpoke in his language; and when he ſpoke (which my father told us, was but ſeldom) it was always in ours.

The

The fix old men, or chiefs, that attended him, defired, after dinner, that the paintings might be produced, and they be permitted to explain them; adding, that his modefty had defired many things to be fuppreffed, which did him equal honour; but that he faid they were only what he had learned from books and obfervations in his own country; and what it gave him the higheft fatisfaction to teach us; for to ferve a nation, whofe whole ftudy confifted in practifing virtue, and excluding vice (in whatever fpecious form it might approach) muft be a delightful tafk, and could deferve no recompenfe.

After this preface, they informed the moft honorable, and the reft of the company, of the tranfactions, in the following manner; the eldeft beginning, and the fecond taking it up, when he was tired, and fo on till the whole had been related.

I

But

But before they began, Woodville begged permiffion to retire; which was granted, by the moft honorable.

' When this hero,' faid the eldeft chief, ' came
' firft amongft us, he found us in the depth of
' mifery—hourly deploring the inroads made
' upon us, by the favage Monoroys, and the
' cruelty of their havock.

' He made many enquiries into the manner of
' our fighting, and of their's, and into the na-
' ture of the weapons each ufed.

' He then defired to be conducted to our
' forges, and workfhops.

' He found them mean, and ill qualified, ei-
' ther by the fkill of the workmen, or nature of
' the works, to produce any ufeful effect.

' He called in the affiftance of his five compa-
' nions; and having obtained our permiffion,
                                        ' they

' they gave such instructions, and shewed them
' by their own performances, the method of ex-
' ecuting them, that in a fortnight's time, our
' store-houses were filled with a variety of wea-
' pons, utterly unknown to us.

' He rose every morning with the sun, and
' taught all that wished to learn the use of these
' new implements of war :——in all, above a
' thousand men became skilled in this unusual
' exercise.

' He then covered pieces of glass, with quick-
' silver, and had them fastened in the front of
' each man's cap or hat.

' Having thus prepared us for war, he taught
' us many useful arts in peace ; but finding our
' bad neighbours were quiet, he desired not to
' molest them ; and told us, he must leave us,
' and go to another nation, as he was to return
' to Camtwell, at the expiration of two springs.

' Two

' Two days after his departure (which
' though we had greatly grieved for, we found
' additional caufe to lament) the inhuman Mo_
' noroys ftole upon us by night ; deftroying,
' in a moft cruel manner, every thing they met
' with, excepting the women and children ;
' whom, to our inexpreffible forrow, they carried
' away with them.

' Our arms were of little ufe ; we were attack-
' ed in the dark, and over powered by numbers ;
' and as we well knew the Monoroys firft ufe the
' women as their barbarous paffions direct, and
' then eat them and the children, our horrors
' were not to be defcribed.

' Luckily fome, who had nothing worth faving
' but their lives, ran away :—one of thefe meet-
' ing with Woodville, gave him the fhocking
' detail of our fufferings.

' The youth, without hefitating a moment,
' mounted his horfe (a kind of deer, fo fierce,
' even

,even he could never manage him, but by blind-
' ing his eyes; and though he would not bear
' the touch of a whip or spur, or even a saddle;
' yet, with his master's stroaking and speaking
' to him, became so gentle as to be guided by a
' slight rein; he loved this creature so much,
' that he has brought him hither) and soon he
' returned to us.

He found me lamenting, with bitter tears and
' lamentations, the captivity of my wife, my
' mother, sister, and four children.

' All he spoke to, had similar misfortunes.

' He shewed us, that our grief, however just,
' would produce no remedy—that could only
' be obtained by our valour; and exhorted all
' who had courage, to follow him.

' He proceeded directly to the store-house of
' our arms and ammunition, followed by a great
' multitude.

' He

' He chofe out five hundred of the ablest, to
' continue under him ;  ordering all the remain-
' der  to  march  different  roads—not  to  attempt
' fighting, if they could avoid it, till all parties
' met ;  faying,  ' The glafs in your caps, will
' enable  you  to  diftinguifh  your  friends  from
' your enemies.

' He defired each man to take bread, &c.
' enough to laft five days.

' He immediately fet forward the direct road,
' with his chofen band.

' The third day, we were in fight of the ene-
' my's chief town ; our detached parties were alfo
' come up to us.

' The enemy poured out by fun rife, the next
' day, in fuch fwarms, as would have terrified us,
' had we not foon found, that our new arms
' faved us from their attack.

' Their

' Their arrows fell harmlefs on our targets;
' whilft our fpears and cutlaffes, created infinite
' havock amongft them.

' But ftill more arrived to fupply the place
' of thofe that fell——amongft this laft body of
' Monoroys, was their king.

' The fun was now high, and fhone out
' bright ;—the reflection from the glafs, almoft
' blinded, and completely terrified them ; fo that
' they threw away their bows, arows, knives
' and hatchets, and fell on their faces.

' We immediately demanded the prifoners ;
' afking, eagerly, if they were fafe.

' They declared, they had not eaten one yet,
' nor had perfuaded one woman to yield to their
' wifhes.

' Our hero, unwilling to deftroy more lives,
' commanded hoftilities to ceafe, in cafe this
                                    ' proved

' proved true; and bid them lead him to the
'' captives, as they were all alive and unhurt.


' He then ordered the enemy's weapons to be
' piled on a heap, and set fire to.


' This done, we entereᵤ ᵢheir city; our hero,
' giving orders that no damage should be done
' to their possessions, nor any outrage committed
' on the person of any of its inhabitants who are
' peaceable.


' This clemency made them look upon us, as
' more than mortal !


' He then ordered all the women and children
' that had been taken from us, to be brought
' forth.


' I should have observed, that before, he had
' taken only their number from our account, and
' gone alone to reckon them; not choosing to
' trust us with the sight of objects so dear to us,
                              ' whilst

'whilst it was possible there might be a necessity
'to avenge the general cause.


'Think, oh! most honorable, and hono-
'rables, that our heads—think what must be the
'joy of each of us, when we again beheld our
'wives, our children, our mothers, and our
'sisters!


'After we had given way to sensations impos-
'sible to be described, our brave warrior came to
'us, saying,


'Let us now determine what is proper to be
'done, to convert your enemies into friends.'


'We all called out with one voice, we would
'be directed by him.


'Then,' cried our brave commander, 'let
'us teach them humanity—let us slaughter no
'more lives; but shew mercy to the poor wretch-
'es, who prove willing to bring in their arms,

I 3                              'and

' and submit to us—let us allow for national
' customs—it is theirs to be cruel—may our ex-
' ample teach them to be humane.

' If any among you can speak their language,
' let them come to me.'

' Two of our men, who could, immediately
' came.

' He ordered them to proclaim, that all who
' would bring their arms, and acknowledge us
.' the conquerors, should be freely pardoned.

' He then commanded all his friends to kneel
' down publicly, and jointly return thanks to
' God for their success.

' The inhabitants of the city, who had been
' clamorous in their screeches and lamentations,
' no sooner heard the proclamation, than they
' were as loud in their praises of the victor's cle-
' mency.

' Immediately

' Immediately they brought us all forts of pro-
' vifions, and a plentiful ftore of drink.

' Moft of us had eaten heartily ; and were juft
' going to quench our thirft, when the two men,
' who had been fent to make proclamation, en-
' tered with the king of the country.

' He directly overturned, or broke all the vef-
' fels that contained the liquor ; and fpoke in a
' very loud tone, and feemingly angry tone,
' to his people.

' He then demanded which was our chief.

' The two men having pointed him out, he
' made an obeifance ; and defired the men to
' explain to us the following fpeech—

' I am thefe wretches' king ; but not the di-
' rector of their bafenefs.

' The army I led out againft you, can all
' witnefs for me, I was ignorant of the mifchief
' the

' the invaders had done in your country, till it
' was too late to prevent it.

' I am now more happy, in arriving time
' enough to prevent the cruel effect of the trea-
' chery intended you.

' 'The liquors, brought you by these bad men,
' under the mask of friendship, were all poifon-
' ed; and had I been ten minutes later, your
' lives would have been facrificed to their bafe
' inhumanity.'

' To prove this he called a dog, and made
' him drink fome of the liquor that was on the
' ground; with horror, we faw him expire in a
' few minutes, in fhocking torments

' The King then called for Zamor, and Guia-
' far; prefenting them to our hero, he faid——

' Thefe are trufty, honeft men—you may
' confide in them :—with me, you may do what
' you pleafe, but ah, fpare my fon !

                                        ' Give

' Give what orders you think proper for your
' safety, and be our friends ; and I think I can.
' anfwer for it, you will not repent it.'

' Whilft he was fpeaking, Zamor and Guiafar
' came with veffels of drink ; prefented fome of
' it to the king, he tafted it, and defired it might
' be given round.

' The two interpreters informed us, that he
' requefted, that for a few minutes, he might
' be permitted to act with the fame authority he
' had formerly done.

' Confent being given, he immediately gave
' orders that every one of thofe ungrateful,
' treacherous wretches, fhould be flain.

' He was directly obeyed.

' They fell, without exciting compaffion, even
' from their fellow citizens : for nature, in its
' uncultivated ftate, abhors treachery and deceit.

' Our

‘ Our friendly king (who had been reinſtated
‘ in the throne, by the clemency of our hero)
‘ told us, by the means of the two interpreters,
‘ that if we could conquer the neighbours on the
‘ right hand of that city, we ſhould have no oc-
‘ caſion to fear any future moleſtation ; and in
‘ gratitude to us he offered to aſſiſt us.

‘ After debating amongſt ourſelves, upon the
‘ wiſdom of the ſcheme, we agreed to undertake
‘ it, if our victorious commander would direct
‘ our plans.

‘ Succeſsful as it proved in the end, it was
‘ very near being fatal to us, to you, and to
‘ mankind ; by being the cauſe of the greateſt
‘ misfortune—the loſs of our brave young leader !

‘ He and two of his moſt intimate compani-
‘ ons, having tired themſelves with walking,
‘ one day lay down to ſleep in a foreſt.

‘ A bear

' A bear iffued out of the thickeft part of it,
' and attacked them with great fury.

' Woodville, though firft and moft hurt,
' ftruck the bear with his cutlafs; this made the
' bear more fierce, and he feverely wounded
' him; but at length, the united efforts of our
' hero, and his companions, deftroyed the fero-
' cious animal.

' But their joy was foon damped, on perceiv-
' ing how much Woodville was hurt, and that
' he was fainting with lofs of blood; when a
' peafant happening to pafs that way, and learn-
' ing the caufe of their diftrefs, ran into the
' wood, with amazing fwiftnefs, and, in a
' fhort time, returned with fome herb of fove-
' reign ufe to ftop bleeding, and heal the moft
' defperate wound.

' He ftamped upon it, and applied it to the
' parts, covered them with a leaf, and bound
' them, fo as to keep on this herb.

' In

' In ten days the wounds were perfectly heal-
' ed; but he was still so weak, from losing so
' large a quantity of blood, that he was obliged
' to continue in that country some time.

' Happy was this accident in the event; for
' by his continuance amongst these savages,
' he civilized them wonderfully;—they loved,
' admired, and obeyed him! calling him by the
' name of the god they worshipped! and being
' willing to adore him as such, he found it there-
' fore an easy matter to settle a peace, productive
' of mutual benefit to all parties.

' But the great difficulty was, to bring these
' savages to bind themselves, in a manner their
' laws made sacred, not to eat human flesh
' again.

' However, when they were convinced, that
' without such vows, Woodville and his friends
' were determined to consider them as enemies,
' they

' they at length confented ; and took their moft
' folemn oath, never more to eat human flefh ;
' and as a proof of their fincerity, they brought
' us all the captives, referved for their barbarous
' feafts :—amongft thefe, was Mr. Chriftopher
' Ware, an Englifhman, who had been fhip-
' wrecked, and fallen into the hands of thefe fa-
' vages.

' Had you feen the joy our commander difco-
' vered at the fight of his countryman, you would
' have melted into tears, as we all did, who
' were prefent.

' One of our paintings will fhew you this
' fcene ; others will alfo fhew his wifdom, va-
' lour, and humanity ; whilft others reprefent
' how kind, and beneficent he has been to us.

' He has taught us to make inftruments that
' will cultivate our lands with lefs labour, and to
                                             ' more

' more advantage ;—he has inftructed us how to
' ufe them.


   ' He has directed us to improve our houfes ;
' and to make fome tenemen's under ground to
' fly to, for a defence againft hurricanes.


   ' He taught a moft ingenious workman to
' make a wonderful machine, to hold a bell;
' which ftrikes the hours, and tells what time it
' is, when we cannot fee the fun.


   ' Many of us underftand his language now,
' as well as we do our own.—But the paintings
' cannot exprefs his mild, humble, and generous
' behaviour to us.


   ' A ftranger would fuppofe he was the obliged,
' and we his benefactors; whereas our greateft
' praife has been, that not one amongft us has
' ever fhewn any envy of him, or ever fpoke a
' word that has not been in his praife.

                                   ' To

' To conclude (though we could go on for
many moons in repeating his merits) it is our
unanimous requeſt, that you, moſt honorable,
the head of all the tribes, will confer the high-
eſt dignity our rules will permit, on the greateſt, and beſt man we ever knew; and that
you will think well of our tribes, for thus returning in ſafety, the moſt uſeful friend, and
kindeſt benefactor; and ſo with wiſhes for
your health and proſperity, and that of the
Ten Tribes, committed to your immediate care,
we take our leaves.'

The ſpeaker ſtopped.

' Such a ſilent attention had been afforded
him, as was ſurpriſing in ſo numerous an audience; but then the applauſe from every mouth,
burſt forth ſo inſtantaneouſly, that nothing dif-
tinctly could be heard, till Emargon, the moſt
honorable, roſe up to ſpeak.

When

When all was hufhed again —

' Say, chiefs, at my defire, that you may
' hear, and report to our friends, how readily
' I comply with their juft requefts ; and what
' pleafure it gives me to find fuch grateful hearts
' in the people committed to my care.'

His greatnefs then ordered Woodville to be
fought for.

As foon as he appeared, the moft honorable
with a becoming ferioufnefs in his countenance,
faid,

' Welcome, thou worthy young man ! —
' young in fprings, but old, very old in every
' virtue that can make a man deferve to be loved
' and honoured, by a virtuous, brave, and free
' people ; who are too noble to envy merit,
' where they find it ; and too honeft to applaud,
' where it is not deferved.

' Such

' Such are the people who require of me, that I fhould reward you to the utmoft of my power.

' You deferve my rank, but as the general voice gave it to me, I hold it as a duty incum- bent upon me, never to part with it; unlefs thofe who gave it, demand it of me; but what I can with honor give, you fhall receive.

' I made you forty years of age, before your return ; I now make you fixty—you can ad- vance but ten more; and can gain thofe only by filling my place.'

Woodville advancing to kifs his hand, Emargon thought he was going to kneel, and drew back ; but obferving his miftake, he faid,

' Pardon me, for fuppofing you ignorant of our rules, which enjoin us to kneel, when children, to our earthly parents ; but when we are grown up, only to our God.—May that Al- mighty Governor of the world, blefs you in

' every

' every virtuous act and defire !—may your own
' parent live to know, and rejoice at the high
' honors you have merited from a generous peo-
' ple, who know how to diftinguifh, and reward
' virtue.'

.The moft honorable then took off his hat, and waving it in the air, gave a fignal for thofe fhouts of joy, which could hardly be reftrained till he had done fpeaking.

Tears were foon obferved, where leaft ex-pected; when Emargon named ' The parent's joy.'

Our hero fhewed a feminine foftnefs, and the tender emotions he felt, for fome minutes choak-ed his voice ; at the fame time, every father wifhed their fon like him.

Recovering his wonted calmnefs, he thanked the moft honorable with the fame modeft grace, that accompanies all his actions.

Emargor

Emargon then gave orders to fit up a houſe ſuitable to Woodville's high dignity; and commanded the paintings that the ſix chiefs had brought, ſhould be conveyed to that repoſitory he had before aſſigned for Woodville's trophies; and then diſmiſſed the aſſembly, that each might end with cheerfulneſs, a day that had given ſo much pleaſure.

We all retired from the moſt honorable's manſion; each one of our tribe invited whom they pleaſed; and Woodville, and his Engliſh friend, accompanied my father and mother, and myſelf, to our abode.

After dinner, we had ſinging and muſic, and concluded the evening with dancing.

My father had requeſted the chiefs that accompanied Woodville, to ſtay that day, and enjoy the jubilee made for the return of their loved hero.

If

of his ferioufnefs, and partake of the feftivity of the day.

The following month was the happieft I had then ever known : I enjoyed the trueft delight an innocent mind can feel in converfing many hours every day, with the fole poffeffor of my heart.

Fleeting hours ! too foon they paffed, and gave way to many painful ones ! for Woodville then declined being fo much at our houfe—feldom joined us in our walks or paftime ; and to me, who knew neither joy or forrow, but as created by him—thofe walks, and paftimes, had no longer power to charm !

My father was almoft conftantly with him ; declaring his fociety was more inftructive, and more pleafing, than any other he could find.

In this way, fix more moons paffed on ; after which, I heard of a plan formed by Woodville,

and

It was pleasant to observe with what surprise they viewed the man, whom they had seen only as an instructor, and a warrior, divest himself and executed by his directions, that was thought the most beneficial, that had ever been known in Youngland; for it remedied the greatest misfortune the country laboured under, which was the want of water.

Three large lakes supplied us with all we had; and the fetching it from thence, was very troublesome.

Woodville convinced our most honourable, that he could, by pipes under ground, convey it to every house; his orders were strictly followed, and the event answered beyond expectation.

The joy and gratitude of all the people was so great, they loaded their benefactor with their most valuable gifts, which were their choicest; feathers, gold, diamonds, and precious stones,

K

they

they fent him an abundance of; not becaufe they thought them valuable enough to be a reward for fo great a fervice as had been done them, but becaufe they underftood they were eftimable in his country.

He received their prefents, with the fame modefty, and gracioufnefs he had ever fhown.

His countryman, having by this time learned, how fatal a longer ftay in our nations would probably prove ; as he was of mature age, when he came amongft us, determined to leave Youngland, and try to return home.

Woodville wifhed to accompany him; my father ftrongly oppofed it, fet before him the dangers, and little probability there was, of his ever reaching his native home.—the only place he preferred to this.

Whilft this matter was in debate, my fufferings were dreadful.

How

How can I relate the dumb forrows of a heart, that had ruined itfelf with love? I had no caufe to reproach myfelf for my choice, indeed, for who could blame me for admiring the moft perfect of the human race?

He poffeffes a wifdom that was unequalled— the moft courageous fpirit, foftened with the gentleft manners; a heart fo pure, that error and falfehood never gained admittance in it; they found no friendly paffion to countenance them; neither could I reproach him; he had taken no pains to win my artlefs love.

My haplefs fituation foon reduced me to a truly pitiable ftate; an unhappy mind, ocafioned a difordered body; and lofs of fleep, and want of appetite, banifhed the rofes from my cheeks; and reduced me to fuch weaknefs, I was unable to leave my room.

Woodville, who had long feen, and grieved for my fufferings; fpent much time with me,

and

and the friend of my youth, my dear Mura; who hardly ever left me.

She had been my loved companion, from the days of childish innocence; she alone had been the confident of my forrows, my joys, my hopes, and my fears!

One day Woodville, finding me alone, seemed for a little time loft in thought; then suddenly roufing himfelf, he took my hand and faid ' my dear Agnes, thou fister of my heart, I muft ' feize this opportunity, to unfold that heart to ' you.

' We are both above deceit, I fcruple the lef ' therefore, to confefs to you, that I am wretch ' ed; not all the honors heaped upon me, car ' mitigate the torment I endure, at feeing my- ' felf the caufe of your illnefs.

' It has been my conftant endeavour, fince ' I perceived your partiality to me, to avoic ' makin

making you unhappy; for this purpofe, I
have, fince my return to Camtwell, frequently abfented myfelf from this loved houfe,. left
I fhould be the means of your ftill refufing
offers, that would be thought worth your ac-
cepting, were you not prepoffeffed in my
favour.

‘ I have gone too far now, not to tell you
every thought of my heart; oh! that your’s
could receive comfort, by reading in that
heart, that it prefers you to every other fair.

‘ From your attachment, and your parent’s
goodnefs, I might hope for every happinefs
arifing from fuch a union; could it be founded on virtue!—But alas, it muft not be;
I muft not wed here! you know my ftory;
you know I have an offended father.

‘ I truft, Heaven and he, will forgive my
fault; but till I am forgiven by him, and reftored his favour, I cannot be happy.

‘ I

' I cannot therefore marry and settle in
' Youngland ;—it would be an ill return to make
' your amiable tendernefs, to give you a runaway,
' whofe confcience is loaded with guilt ; who
' would, though bleft with you, hourly feel the
' reproaches of his own mind.

' I cannot therefore ftay here!——I cannot
' forfake the wife who loves me ; neither can I
' refolve to give up for ever, the father I have of-
' fended !

' Pity me, my dear Agnes! let the love of
' truth, which infpires us both, operate fo, as
' to prevent your blaming me, if I have been
' too prefumptuous in fuppofing myfelf fo dear
' to you.

' I almoft wifh I may have been fo ; as then,
' you will comply with your friends wifhes, and
' unite with fome equally worthy, and more
' happy man !

' I

' I confefs to you, your parents and I have
' often converfed on this topic; they fee, and
' feel for my fufferings; confult with them;
' let their counfel direct you.

' Oh! may it teach you to find more happi-
' nefs than can be enjoyed by me, who am con-
' fidered as the moft fortunate, and bleft of mor-
' tals; alas! how little do they guefs the mife-
' ries I endure!

' If my peace of mind is dear to you, endea-
' vour to regain your health and fpirits ;—make
' a noble effort—an effort worthy of your piety,
' your tendernefs for your parents, and your ex-
' alted underftanding.

' The greatnefs of your mind, fhould not
' fhrink under difficulties !—'

At this inftant, his voice faultered ;—he ftopped fpeaking, and his eyes met mine—both were
filled with tears—I could fpeak no other language, than thofe too expreffive tears.

He

He silently, and tenderly kissed my hand, and instantly rushed out of the room.

My mother hearing him go hastily away, came directly to me :—she found me in a passion of grief, I could not restrain—she tenderly soothed my sorrows—sat with me till I went to bed; giving me some drops, to compose my frame.

About two hours after the family were at rest, we heard a dreadful noise, and were soon alarmed by the cry of fire !

I opened my eyes, and saw the flames bursting into my room !

I threw on a loose gown, and hastily ran to the window---I was trying to open it, with a design to fling myself out, when I found myself caught by somebody behind me, and hastily carried away.

I fainted in the arms of my supporter, without knowing who it was that saved my life.

How

CHARLES MANDEVILLE.

How long I remained infenfible, I know not ;
but the firft objeɛt that prefenteḍ itfelf to my returning fight, was my beloved Mura : I looked
with an anxious enquiring countenance, yet
dared not enquire.

She, who had long been able to read my
thoughts, faid,

‘ Let us be thankful, my dear Agnes, no lives
‘ are loft !—all are happily, and wonderfully
‘ preferved !’

‘ Oh! tell me,’ I cried, ‘ all you know of
‘ this fad difafter.

‘ Where are my parents ? where am I ? how
‘ came I here ?’

‘ Your mother gave you a compofing draught,
‘ as fhe dreaded the effeɛts of your agitation in
‘ your weak ftate ;—this lulled your forrows to
‘ reft ;—but poor Woodville's kept him waking ;
‘ which has been the means of our preferva-
‘ tion.

K 3                           ‘ He

' He and his friend were walking at midnight,
' in the grove ; talking over the subject that
' diſtreſſed his mind ; when they obſerved an
' unuſual light from your father's houſe.

' They were ſoon convinced it was on fire,
' and flew to aſſiſt ; but the flames had increaſed
' ſo much, ere they reached it, that it was with
' difficulty they could get to the chambers.

' The ſtranger brought out your mother ; ànd
' Woodville ruſhed through the fire to ſave you.

' He overtook me, with you, ſeemingly dead
' in his arms.

' He ſtopped my cries, by aſſuring me you
' were in a ſwoon ; but as his houſe was too far
' off, he propoſed entering this houſe, which
' we found empty ; for all the inhabitants had
' left the neighbouring houſes, fearing the fire
' would extend to them ; and, ſuch as were able,
' were themſelves employed in trying to extin-
' guiſh the flames.

                                        ' When

‘ When Woodville faw your fenfes returning,
‘ he told me he fhould leave you to my care, as
‘ he might be of more ufe elfewhere.

‘ About an hour ago, I heard voices, and
‘ people walking in the houfe ;—feeing a light
‘ in the next room, I opened the door, and faw
‘ Moina (Hubert's fifter) there ; fhe told me fhe
‘ was coming to fupply my place, and fit by you,
‘ requefting I would go to her bed.

‘ I confented to half her defire, as I wifhed
‘ to enquire into the particulars of the fire.

‘ I begged her to ftay in the room with you,
‘ and went myfelf into the hall, from whence
‘ the voices came.

‘ There I found your Father, Woodville,
‘ Ware, Hubert, and many others, all re-
‘ joicing in the happy effects of Woodville's late-
‘ ly executed plan of conveying water ; which
‘ had now been the means of putting out the fire,
‘ before any confiderable damage was done ;
                                        ‘ whereas

' whereas formerly, one houfe was feldom left,
' when once fuch a misfortune happened.

' They praifed him for his active vigilance
' and care in directing the men; fo that only
' three houfes had fuffered.

' I learned alfo, that your mother was fafe at
' her brother's houfe, having only fuffered from
' terrors for you; and when fhe had been inform-
' ed of your fafety, confented to remain there.

' Hearing that every thing was far better than
' I could have hoped, I returned to you, whofe
' reafon I found was returning; therefore I in-
' fifted on Moina's leaving you to my care, as I
' was unwilling fhe fhould be a witnefs to the
' effufions of your heart—that heart which will,
' I hope, now be eafy.'

' Alas! my Moira,' fa'd I, ' eafe will never
' be my lot! but I muft not repine :—God has
' been very merciful to us—his will be done;
                                                ' yet

' yet too true it is, painful days, and fleeplefs
' nights, will be my fate for many a day, ere I
' regain my loft tranquility; but my patient fub-
' miffion fhall fhow, I can love and fuffer much,
' yet ftill love on.

' May my recompenfe be found in Wood-
' ville's being happy! oh, may he never feel
' my forrows:

' Blefs him, oh! thou Almighty Power, in
' every wifh his worthy heart can form!'

Oppreffed with my grief and weaknefs, I fell
into a found fleep—waked revived, and with a
cheerfulnefs I had not felt for fome time; took
fome refrefhment, and rofe, alas, to experience
frefh forrows!

I faw all my friends, excepting him my heart
moft wifhed to fee.

Ah, I did not then know the extent of my
woe! him I muft not fee; for my evil deftiny
had

had contrived, that the houfe he had carried me to, was Hubert's!—a fingle man—a rejected lover—I had ftayed there all night!

Too foon I learned the horrors of my fate—this accident gave him a right to demand me in marriage:—he immediately claimed his right of my father.

. My tender parents told me of this additional misfortune; adding, I knew the indifpenfable rules of our nation; gave me no other choice, but to wed Hubert, or to leave my father's houfe, and go into the clafs of ' ufeful employments,' within a fortnight; which time was allowed me, to make my option.

I hefitated not one moment which to fix upon! Death would have been preferable to the mar-rying of any man but Woodville.

I went back to my parent's home, for the al-lotted time; but never was allowed to fee the object my foul doted on.

He

He wrote to me every day; not as a lover, but as a friend and brother.

His eloquence was prevalent ; he reafoned fo juftly, and yet fo tenderly, that he infpired me with fortitude ; and I left my father's houfe, with more compofure, than could be expected.

The branches of bufinefs I chofe, (for all have power to chufe) were painting and embroidery.

Thefe occupations amufed my mind, and I by degrees regained my health.

Woodville was then permitted to vifit me often ; for the rules of this clafs do not prohibit fociety ; they forbid a perfon from fleeping from home, but allow them to fee their friends ; and permit them to marry, either one of the fame clafs ; or if of a fuperior clafs, a perfon not lefs than thirty years old.

But then, the head of the clafs is to be confult- ed, inftead of the maiden's father ; for the head is to be efteemed as the father, who lofes all pa- ternal

ternal right over his child, after entered the clafs
of ' ufeful employments.'

My hours were lefs painful than I could have
expected.

My love was not leffened; but time had taught
me refignation ; and by never allowing myfelf
to be idle, I learned to bear my lot without mur-
muring.

When one dear bleffed day, my beloved
Woodville entered, with an unufual cheerfulnefs
in his countenance.

He told me (oh! joyful found! it ftill vi-
brates on my ear) ' that the head of that clafs
' had gratified his ardent defire; and that he
' hoped, I would not be againft his being happy!'

' I againft it! faid I; ' no! furely your hap-
' pinefs is the firft wifh of my heart.

' If you are going to marry, may the happy
' maiden love you as I have done; if fhe can
                                    ' do

' do it farther, I am ftill ignorant of the power of
' love.

' Long as I have been its votary, my comfort,
' in all my forrows, has been, that I have not
' hurt your glory.

' Shall I now wifh to hinder your happinefs ?

' Ah! Agnes' faid the dear youth,. ' have
' you fo little penetration, as to think my peace
' of mind can be reftored, by a union with any
' other woman but yourfelf ? nay, even with
' you, can I hope it will be perfect ; for do I
' not labour under misfortunes, which, not all
' the honors this dear country have loaded me
' with, can efface ? nay, fhall I not add to
' them ?

' I have robbed my own father of his eldeft
' fon; and fhall rob your's of his only child ;
' for furely, when you fo generoufly wifhed hap-
' pinefs to the wife I chofe, you did not recollect,
' you muft be that wife !

May

' May thofe wifhes light on your own dear
' head! for you, Agnes! are the only woman
' fhall tempt me to unite in a foreign land.

' Yet I tremble for the event; as I fear the
' conditions of our union, may wound your
' peace of mind: but I love truth, as much as
' I do my Agnes.

' I muft not therefore deceive you!

' Ware fets out in three days, to endeavour
' to regain Europe!—If he is happy enough to
' fucceed, he fends a fhip for me.

' Now, Agnes, decide my fate; weigh well
' your own determination! can your affection
' for me, be great enough to compenfate for the
' quitting your parents, your friends, and your
' country! and reconcile you to many hardfhips,
' it may be, even my tendernefs cannot fhield
' you from, ere we reach my native land?

' Confider

‘ Confider the fubjeƈt thoroughly, and forgive
‘ the prefumption that arifes from my fincerity,
‘ in propofing conditions to the beloved of my
‘ foul !’

‘ Oh! my heart's beft treafure ! it requires
‘ no time to confider and weigh the matter !

‘ I am willing to be your wife, to fhare with
‘ you every danger, and difficulty ! you are
‘ parents, friends, and country to me,—but
‘ is it poffible, that you, who are now arrived
‘ to the dignity of an honorable of fixty years,
‘ can condefcend to take me, degraded as I am !
‘ no longer to be confidered as the daughter of
‘ an honorable, but as one of the clafs, fo much
‘ beneath their honors ?’

‘ Call not yourfelf by fo undeferved an epithet !
‘ fay exalted, not degraded !

‘ The noblenefs of your choice did, indeed,
‘ exalt you in my eftimation ; highly as I be-
‘ fore thought of your merits.’

But

But it would be as vain for me to attempt to repeat one half of the kind, the tender things he said, as to endeavour to recite half his virtues.

He told me, that though our rule difpenfed with the natural parents confent, to marry a maiden in my prefent fituation; yet, as with fubmiffion to our laws, he thought nothing ought to deprive the parent of his power over his child; he had previoufly confulted my father and mother, and gained their approbation, before he addreffed the head of the clafs, for leave to marry me.

He alfo informed me, that he feared he fhould not be able to fee me the two following days, as they muft be given up to his friend, in order to fit him out as well as poffible, for fo defperate a journey, as made him fhudder for him, as well as for himfelf; fince, upon Ware's fuccefs depended his future hope of returning to England.

At

At the expiration of that time, he came to me, told me his friend was gone, and all things getting ready for our nuptials.

The neceffary preparations completed, my lover, and the head of the clafs, fummoned me to church.

The golden chain encircled us amidft our furrounding friends; amongft which, my parents were not the leaft joyful.

The ceremony over—I was led,—oh! joyful moments! to my hufband's houfe! and received the congratulations of every perfon, with a heart fully at eafe.

Here I lived the happieft of women; for to complete my felicity, Hubert had withdrawn his affections from me, and placed them, where they were moft acceptable, and moft deferved.

On

On the friend of my heart, my dear Mura; who had long secretly loved him, concealing her attachment even from me, till I had made my choice, and by quitting my father's house, plainly evinced, I never would be the wife of Hubert !

The week after the birth of my little Charles, the moft honorable, the good Emargon, died— full of years and honors.

The voices that were to elect his fucceffor, were unanimous to place my Woodville in the vacant feat.

He received the account with gratitude ; but declined the intended honor; proving to the ancients and the fires, the impropriety of giving the moft honorable place to a ftranger ; to one too, who muft confefs, he would, when ever opportunity offered, return to his native land.

Though

Though whilſt he ſta ed, and to his life's end, he would make it his ſtudy to deſerve the many favors they had ſhewn him.

His all perſuaſive eloquence prevailed, greatly as they wiſhed otherwiſe.

They then proceeded to a new election ; and with one conſenting voice, choſe my father ; not only, they ſaid, on account of his own merit, but as he had been the ultimate cauſe of the bene-fits they had received from Woodville, by the preſervation of him ; and as he was now ſo cloſely connected with him, their beloved bene-factor.

Shouts of joy proclaimed their choice ; and with the cuſtomary forms, my father was inveſ-ted with the moſt honorable's authority.

Our happineſs hourly increaſed ; a ſecond boy was added to our bleſſings,——but alas ! human joys are not permanent !

A ſickneſs,

A ficknefs, often fatal to infants, fnatched away both our babes, in three months time, and I fhould have nearly funk under my grief, but for the neceffity I was under, to roufe myfelf, in order to keep up my dear hufband's fpirits; who grew penfive and almoft melancholy; often telling me, ' he looked upon himfelf, as the pri-' mary caufe of our misfortune.

' Believing, that Divine goodnefs had be-
' reaved him of his children, in order to imprefs
' him more ftrongly with a fenfe of his own
' crime, in forfaking a father, who might, per-
' haps, now want his filial tendernefs, to footh
' his cares, in a country, in which, it is true,
' there was more improved knowledge, than in
' our's; yet, as he muft own, there was much
' more vice; fo he proved, there were alfo many
' more afflictions.'

My utmoft endeavours were ufed to banifh fuch cruel thoughts, and revive his fpirits: that amiable temper, which delighted to make others happy,

happy, made him exert his own efforts, that my affiduity might be fuccefsful; and, at length, I had the happinefs of feeing his natural vivacity return.

One morning my father fent for him; in the evening when he returned, I obferved a cheerfulnefs in his looks, that told me fome event joyous to him had happened; and I foon caught the livelinefs, his eyes expreffed; as my heart was ever in unifon with his.

He tenderly embraced me, faying, ' Oh! my ' Agnes, you fhould love me lefs; or the tor-
' rent of felicity that daily pours upon me, will ' overwhelm me, and make me forget that I am ' mortal!

' But I fear, I fhall check the fympathizing ' joy that has lighted up your features, with ' ftill more than ufual brightnefs, when I tell ' you, the fource of my prefent fatisfaction arifes

L                                     ' from

' from the profpect of returning home to my na-
' tive land!

 

' Letters are arrived from Ware, informing
' the moft honorable, which he fuppofes to be
' Emargon ftill, that he has been happy enough
' to reap the good effects of civilizing barbari-
' ans, and converting enemies into friends.

 

' Our letters of recommendation, conducted
' him fafely to the nation nearest Youngland.

 

' Their chief recommended him to the next;
' and fo he was paffed on for eight hundred miles,
' meeting with every kindnefs which humanity
' could fhew, or his fituation require.

 

' At the end of this journey he met with a
' veffel, which carried him fafe to an Englifh
' fettlement; from whence he could, with eafe,
' proceed to England, with every reafonable af-
' furance of a profperous voyage.

' He

' He adds, at the end of which, he fhould en-
' deavour to turn to the beft advantage for
' me, the treafures he had been trufted with.


' I did not underftand the meaning of this
' fentence; well knowing, that all he had re-
' ceived from me, were fome prefents to himfelf, .
' which I had added to the fplendid ones which
' had been given to him by the moft honorable,
' and honorables : but that my 'obligations to
' this generous nation may be hourly increafing,
' I foon learned, that Emargon, your father, and
' many others, had found means,' by fending a
' veffel round the coaft, to meet Ware, at the
' fhip fide ; and that this veffel had been ftored
' with ingots of pure gold, diamonds, and moft
' precious gems ; with orders to difpofe of them
' in the manner moft likely to turn out for my
' benefit, in cafe I ever reached home ; allowing
' him to referve the fourth part to himfelf ; and
' defiring him, if my father was living, to give
' the remainder to him, for my ufe, if I ever re-
' turned home.

' Thus,

' Thus, you fee, my deareft treafure, the
' bounty of our friends will make us rich in my
' native country.

' But now, my dear Agnes, comes the trial
' of your love, and of your courage !

' In ten months Ware hopes I fhall find a
' fhip, at a particular river he has named ; which
' will be fent on purpofe to convey me from
' hence—may I flatter myfelf, you can cheer-
' fully accompany me ?'

' May you ! how can you wound me by im-
' plying a doubt ? are we not linked for life ?
' fhall I not partake of whatever heaven allots to
' you ?—let me ftill be dear to you, and do not
' forfake me, or deprive me of that affection
' which makes my life a blefling ; and then, be
' affured, I fhall find nothing a hardfhip in your
' loved fociety.'

He preffed me to his heart in tranfport, faying.

' Thou

' Thou art the only treasure I shall wish to
' carry away; all others are but as a feather,
' compared with thee!'

As soon as I had recovered the birth of that
sweet babe, who has been the companion of our
journey, we began to prepare for our departure

Soon after the time our friend had fixed,
we received intelligence, that the ship was arrived.

Woodville called all his dependants—told them
the time he intended to remove, and offered them
any service in his power with the honorables, as
a reward for their fidelity.

Two young women, two men, and two boys,
requested to accompany us; and live or die with
us.

Woodville told them, they must first obtain
                                        their

their parents, and the moſt honorable's con-
ſent.

This was readily granted :—the whole nation
would have been truſted to his care, could they
have been removed.

The laſt day we went to our church, we found,
on the outſide of the repoſitory, aſſigned to
Woodville's trophies, the following inſcrip-
tion.

' To-morrow, being the third of the fourt
' month, in the ſix hundred and fourth ſpring o
' this ſettlement, we are to be deprived of Wood-
' ville, the oldeſt young man we ever ſaw ; and
' the greateſt benefactor to our nation, as well as
' the very beſt man it has ever known.

' He was truth itſelf! a falſhood never iſſued
' from his lips ; nor was a deceit ever practiſed
' by him.

He

He was wife without vanity; brave without rafhnefs; compaffionate without weaknefs; had dignity without pride; and his delight has been to do good to all, though his modefty would not let him take all the honorable rewards that he fo well deferved.

' His manners adorn virtue in himfelf; and his example teaches it to others.

' Filial tendernefs, that moft valuable of all the affections of the human mind, has fhewn itfelf predominant in him——it has prevailed over intereft, ambition, and all that could charm, or entice a mortal; and it has obliged him to return home, to receive a father's blef-fing! but, alas! it robs Youngland of their god-like benefactor.

' When far diftant, he will ftill remain in their hearts—his praifes will flow from their lips; and their prayers fhall be offered to Hea-for his fafety.

' This

' This writing !—an art he himfelf taught firft
' —fhall tranfmit to future generations, an ac-
' count of the bleffings he procured to Young-
' land.'

Then followed the lift of all the benefits he had
conferred on the country.

My modeft Woodville will not let me enume-
rate thefe benefits ; they are more than can be
conceived.

After Woodville had, with tears in his eyes,
perufed this writing, he turned to his furrounding friends—thanked them for all their generous
goodnefs to him ; affured them, their welfare,
and the profperity of their nation, fhould ever be
an object to him, however diftant he might be ;
and, as a proof of it, if he ever obtained any influence in his own country, he would exert it,
to fend them fuch a holy man, as their painting
delineated (with feveral copies of that facred boc'

called the bible) to inftruct them in the rites of Chriftianity.

They already practifed the dictates of the Chriftian Religion; and till that clergyman arrived amongft them, the beft advice he could give them, was to adhere ftrictly to their own rules, as thofe rules taught every virtue which could adorn human nature!

After more difcourfe, and the ufual repetition of the Lord's prayer, creed, and ten commandments, the people fung a hymn, made for the occafion, expreffive of their earneft wifhes for his happinefs and fafety.

He had been apprifed of this intention, and had been prepared to return it; having compofed a hymn, in which myfelf, and twelve more he had felected, were to join him.

This hymn, which repeated his gratitude, and prayed for bleffings on this nation, was thought

the

the fineſt piece of muſic which had ever been heard there ; where he himſelf (who has the moſt harmonious voice that ever ſung) thought the muſic was ſuperior to any he had ever heard in England.

Happy ſhall I be, if ever it is allowed me, to ſing this hymn to his father !

My parents were not able to ſee us the laſt day ; but ſhut themſelves up, and prayed for bleſſings on their children.

However, they ſhewed ſo much fortitude, as not to utter a wiſh to detain us.

I requeſted the friend of my heart—my dear Mura, to follow their example, and avoid the agonizing farewell ! for I dreaded every thing that could enervate me, and of courſe render me leſs able to encounter the painful moment of my departure !

Indeed,

Indeed, I found occasion for my utmost refolution to support my own spirits, that I might not
deprefs my beloved's; whofe tender heart felt for
me, as well as for his own leaving, for ever, a
country he had fo many reafons to love !

Hubert, and many other friends, accompanied us to the water fide.

Every thing had been planned with fo much
care, and every plan was fo well executed, that
our land journey was performed in eight days,
with very little fatigue, and without diftrefs or
danger.

Our fhip was then loaded with immenfe treafures, as this country calls them.

The kind folicitude of my hufband (lover I may
ftill call him, for fuch he has continued, ever
fince I have been his happy wife) fo alleviated
every anxiety, and increafed every comfort, that
the voyage proved only a pleafant expedition ;
　　　　　　　　　　　　　　　　　　　and

and the care of my fweet child, and writing thefe memoirs, fo filled up my time, that I had no wifh for fociety in thofe hours my Woodville could not devote to me!

We were met, at the firft Englifh fettlement by Mr. John Ware, (a brother of our friend's, who lives abroad; he had taken charge of difpo-fing of part of the gold and jewels Mr. Chrif-topher Ware had brought from my dear father, and the honorables, for our ufe; as it was thought moft prudent to convert them into the fpecies of this country, in different plaçes.)

This gentleman ftaid with us there for one month, and then accompanied us to Amfter-dam; where we were to meet his brother, and fettle our affairs.

We learned, by Mr. John Ware's account, that what had been already brought from Young-land, produced an immenfe property in England: a circumftance I heard with pleafure (though not

grown

grown more avaricious) as I had already feen enough to make me think, that in the mother country (as my beloved always calls it) wealth was in as great eftimation as virtue ! or, at leaft, that virtue without riches, would be but little efteemed !

I could not help faying to myfelf—I knew a more happy count y, where merit alone was valued ; and where an additional feather, acquired by noble actions, would render the wearer more honoured, than all the gems and gold in the world ; as thofe might be gained by a thoufand accidents, in which the merit of the owner was not concerned ; but the honorable feather muft be obtained by real defert.

A figh, and a tender tear, accompanied this mental reflection ; but the feeing Woodville ap-proach, made me fupprefs every painful idea.

His loved prefence can, at any time, diffi-pate concern that I would carefully hide from him ;

him ; left he fhould fuppofe I repented the having left my country, and my friends !——a
fuppofition his tendernefs would be alarmed at,
but I can moft truly fay, it would be groundlefs :
——in him, and my beloved child, are center-
ed all my ideas of happinefs.

Next week, it was intended, we fhould proceed on our journey to England—but, alas, I
find my journies in this world are over !

I am feized with an illnefs, they call the
fmall pox, and am convinced it will prove fatal !

I refign my life with gratitude, for the many
bleffings I have enjoyed, into the hands of him
who gave it !

My confcience tells me, I have lived innocent-
ly, and I hope to die happy.

                                        I am

I am fatisfied in the belief, my dear infant will be taken true care of, by the tendereft of fathers——he will love her for my fake !

I wifhed to have feen his father, but the Almighty's will be done !

May the Power above protect, and fhield from every ill, the moft worthy of mankind !

May he meet with every bleffing in his own country, that can atone for thofe he has left; and leffen that forrow I am certain he will feel on my account !

I hope to live long enough to deliver thefe papers into the hands of Mr. Chriftopher Ware, who is hourly expected from London ; as I well know the modefty of my amiable hufband, would fupprefs an account which does fo much credit to himfelf.

I wifh

I wifh his neareft friends fhould fee it ; and I requeft of them to believe, I honor truth too much, to infert one falfity !

## Conclusion of Mrs. Mandeville's Memoirs.

To

To Mr. HERBERT.

THE immenfe packets that have been tranf-
mitted to you, by Colonel Belville's pen, have
permitted mine to fleep in peace.

Indeed I think you would have been vexed,
with any interruption, in the perufal of fuch interefting papers.

I almoft wifh I had never read them, for I cannot help lamenting, that the amiable writer of
them, was not herfelf the bearer to us!—and,
highly as I efteem Emily, I think fhe will have a
of a man who appear to advantage, as the wife
nes.

Her

Her character feems to me, to be as perfect in its way, as his; and we all fhed tears, when we perufed her affecting elofe of her memoirs.

Emily wept, very fincerely, I dare fay; yet I could not help thinking, fhe would have fhed more painful tears, had the fweet Agnes ftill been living.

My time has been, as ufual, employed in trying to cheer the finking fpirits of my friends.

The thoughts of the approaching trials, opened every wound afrefh! It has called Lord Belmont, and Colonel Mandeville away.

They departed with heavy hearts leaving us to the care of Mr. Mandeville; who has endeavoured, by every tender affiduity, to banifh mournful reflections from more comfort from his and in company, than I thought fhe would ever know again.

Her

Her fondnefs for him daily increafes; nor can one be furprized at it, as each day he difcovers fome new art of pleafing.

Sure no one man was ever endued with fo many powers to delight every age and fex! I am fometimes out of humour, that I cannot difcover one fault, to bring him more upon the level with ourfelves; his voice is melody itfelf.

Well might poor Agnes fay, it exceeded all fhe had ever heard; I was told in Italy, I had been entertained by the fineft voices in the world; but I am convinced they were miftaken; they had never heard Mr. Mandeville's!—his folemn hymns, make you believe you are liftening to more than mortal founds, his cheerful fongs animate your whole foul, and leave you not a thought or idea that is not joyous!

I learn this day, from the happy Emily, that he has gained her permiffion, when hisfather and my lord return, to afk their confent to her becoming his bride.

I think

I think it will be joyfully given, and then our ftory will be properly wound up; the gay widow will foon be converted into the fober wife; the blufhing maiden, into the prudent matron; and as my vein for letter writing is worn out, I can the eafier condefcend to the dull narration of domeftic fcenes; which, though they may be very delightful in the acting, make but an infipid figure in the recital.

I truft we fhall have no more mad rencounters, to create tragic fubjects for my pen: but be content to admire the mercy of Providence, who has thus healed the forrows of a worthy family, by reftoring its loft branches! adorned with every fruit that can make it valuable!

The great bell announces vifitors, fo for the prefent. Adieu!

(IN CONTINUATION.)

Laft Thurfday Lord Belmont, and the Colonel
returned:

returned : their countenances betrayed the dejection of their hearts.

Lord Melvin was acquitted, as every body knew he muft be ; my Lord dwelled no longer on the painful fubject, than to do juftice to the manly tendernefs, and deep concern, Lord Melvin expreffed on the fad occafion.

Mr. Mandeville led the difcourfe into topics, lefs painfully interefting to the company.

After tea, he requefted his father to walk with him : Emily's blufhes were tell tales, that fhe knew the fubject he meaned to difcufs.

Colonel Mandeville has enabled me to give you the particulars of their converfation.

The Colonel, on hearing his fon's wifhes, faid, ' I am not furprized ; as I thought, I pret-
' ty early difcovered your partiality for Mifs How-
' ard :

' ard : which gave me great pleafure, as I know
' her to be a truly amiable girl.'

' Oh ! fir, you might indeed fee it, on the
' firft of my acquaintance with her ; nay, on my
' firft fight of her, had you been prefent ; for
' never were two fifters more like each other,
' than Mifs Howard is, to my dear Angel !

' This ftrong refemblance led me to obferve
' her character and difpofition ; the more I ftu-
' died them, the likenefs ftrengthened ; the fame
' modeft diffidence, the fame fweet feminine
' foftnefs, that my beloved Agnes poffeffed, ap-
' pear in all Mifs Howard fays or does ; they feem
' to be reuniting to the woman I adored ;—
' and in her, I hope to find a fecond fond mo-
' ther for my dear girl !

' I hope, fir, you have formed no views for
' me, that this attachment interferes with.'

' From me, child, you fhall never meet with
' any

' any obftruction to your wifhes ;—I hope it will
' alfo receive my Lord's approbation—but of this
' I am not fo certain.'

' Why, fir, I am not confcious of any ground
' for objection to my propofal.'

' Lord Belmont, my dear Charles, is a man
' of nice honor—perhaps, too punctilious in
' fome matters ; and, though I really think that
' every action of your life, does credit to you ;
' he, perhaps, may fee in a different light, your
' early elopement, and the ftate of dependence
' you were once in.'

' I have not fullied my honor, and, therefore,
' do not expect contempt from any man ; efpe-
' cially from a man of my Lord's good fenfe.

' If I find it, I can only fay, I had rather be
' again the menial dependent I once was, than
' be his lordfhip ; for till I can be convinced a
' coronet adds worth to the heart of its wearer,
                                                    ' I can

‘ I can only confider it as the ornament of the
‘ head.’


‘ I hope, my dear Charles, you judge more
‘ truly of him, in this matter, than I do—I
‘ thought it proper to guard you againſt a diſ-
‘ appointment that might lead you into improper
‘ warmth; all men have ſome ſhade in their cha-
‘ racters; this is the only one in his; and it
‘ cannot overcaſt the bright ſunſhine of virtues
‘ that illuminate his mind.


‘ As to myſelf, I am much pleaſed with your
‘ choice; but had I not been ſo, I would not
‘ have thwarted your inclinations; let me once
‘ be bleſſed with a boy of your’s, and I ſhall for-
‘ get my paſt ſufferings; they have been ſo great
‘ ſince my poor Harry’s untimely end, that I
‘ think I could not long have ſupported myſelf
‘ under them, had not the unexpected bleſſing I
‘ now enjoy, cheered my ſad heart !’


Mr. Mandeville, willing to give his thoughts
another

another fubject, took a paper out of his pocket book; prefenting it to his father, faying, ' you ' told me, fir, I need not fear having more riches ' than I could fpend, in this country ; be fo kind ' to perufe this fchedule of my fortune, and you ' will find it too much for any man !'

' The Colonel read, ' received, from Mr. Ware ' feventy thoufand pounds, the firft payment ; ' the fecond, thirty thoufand ; the third, for ' jewels and ingots of gold, brought by himfelf, ' and difpofed of by Mr. Chriftopher Ware, fifty ' thoufand ; the produce of the newly arrived ' fhips, two hundred thoufand pounds ; feventy ' thoufand laid out in land, by Mr. John Ware, ' before Mr. Mandeville arrived.'

The Colonel then turned the paper, and continued reading a plan Mr. Mandeville had laid down, for the difpofal of his fortune.

His fon repeated, ' I think fir, you will ac-
                    M                    ' knowledge

' nowledge this is too much wealth for any man
' to poſſeſs.'

' For any man but you, I ſhould think it was;
' but this ſcheme for your future conduct, ſhews
' me you will confer credit on your riches; in-
' ſtead of deriving it from them!

' May God bleſs you, with comforts in pro-
' portion to your benevolent intentions.'

' You will perceive, ſir, that my plan extends
' to but one half of my poſſeſſions; the other
' half, I conſider as your property, not mine;
' and devote it entirely to your diſpoſal.

' If you find it more than your inclination al-
' lows you to ſpend upon your own occaſions,
' your better judgment, and greater knowledge
' of this country, will enable you to find out
' worthy ſubjects to beſtow it on; to raiſe de-
' preſſed and ſuffering virtue, will make it turn
' to a ſolid advantage.

' Of

' Of the fhare I have referved to myfelf, I
' fhould be forry not to dedicate a large portion
' to thefe purpofes.

' I fhall ftill have enough left, to gratify all
' my defires :—the pomp and fhew of wealth,
' cannot, in my opinion, increafe the happinefs
' of its owner.'

With eyes and heart overflowing with grateful
joy, the Colonel embraced his excellent fon : ex-
claiming,

' Oh! it is too, too much, my child, for an
' old man to fupport fuch a tide of joy, as you
' pour in upon me !'

After fome more difcourfe, they feparated,—
each of them delighted! the fon, that he had
been happy enough to revive his drooping father,—the father, that he was bleffed with fuch a
fon.

M 2

When

When they returned to the company, their countenances were animated by thefe pleafing fenfations.

This morning a meffenger has arrived from Lady Mary, juft as Mr. Mandeville had enquired of me, if Lord Belmont was gone to his library, as he wifhed to find him alone ; and a fervant had informed Mr. Mandeville, Lord Belmont requefted to fpeak with him.

I confefs myfelf apprehenfive, there may be fome fcheme in agitation between my Lord and his fifter, that may interfere with the Honorable's wifhes.

When amongft ourfelves, we frequently call him by his foreign appellation; but he prefers, he fays, the name ever dear to him ; though fo long laid afide ; but now reaffumed, with fincere and grateful joy.

Lady Belmont has juft left me ; and given me leave to tranfmit to you the particulars of

the

the library converſation, which ſhe had learned from his Lordſhip.

I am ſo tired of ' he ſaid,' and Mr. Man-
' deville replied,' that though I am not going to write a farce, yet I will put it into dramatis perſonæ.

Lord Belmont.——I wanted, Mr. Mandeville, to inform you of my wiſhes, that you would ac-company me, to wait upon my ſiſter Lady Mary.

I am anxious to introduce you to her ; but a letter this morning, tells me, ſhe propoſes com-ing hither to-morrow, to congratulate us all on your return :—a return, ſo happy for each, but moſt peculiarly ſo to me ; who am now no long-er at a loſs for an heir to my fortune and my honors ; they will devolve on you, and I rejoice they will be poſſeſſed by a man every way worthy of them !

Mr.

Mr. Mandeville.—Forgive me, my Lord, if I am incapable of expreſſing my ſentiments of gratitude, as I ought to do ; I feel, at this moment, the misfortune of my education ; but my actions, I hope, will do more credit to my feelings than my language can.

The chief merit that I boaſt, is a ſincerity which, whether nature gave me or not, muſt have been acquired, in a country, where it is conſidered as the firſt of virtues! your Lordſhip's kindneſs makes me hope, I ſhall be forgiven a requeſt, I intended to make to you to day ; a requeſt which that ſame ſincerity makes it improper, in my opinion, to conceal any longer.

Lord Belmont.—Speak it freely; I think I can ſafely promiſe ; you can aſk nothing of me, I ſhall be unwilling to comply with.

Mr. Mandeville.——Thus emboldened by your goodneſs, may I hope for your permiſſion, to addreſs Miſs Howard ?—I freely acknowledge

to

to your Lordſhip, without an union with her, neither wealth or titles can make me happy.

Lord Belmont.—Honeſtly ſpoke my dear Charles, oh! had your poor brother been equally open, in divulging his wiſhes, we might all have been happy! but God's will be done! I was myſelf to blame!—However, it is vain to reflect on what is paſt! we muſt endeavour, by ſubmiſſion to the decrees of Providence, to atone for our errors: remembering, that if we were never to meet with adverſity, we ſhould be too apt to forget our abode in this world, is only deſigned as preparatory to a better.

My Lord then propoſed acquainting Lady Belmont with the ſubject they were upon; adding, I fancy you want no advocate in Emily's heart; but if you ſhould, I am miſtaken if her Ladyſhip does not prove a willing one.

Mr. Mandeville ſaid, you will be ſo kind, as

to

to let my father know, your wishes about settle-
ment.

Lord Belmont.——I will talk them over with
you; for on this occasion I must represent your
father; he cannot spare a great deal, and shall
not lessen his income; mine is sufficient to allow me to divide part with you.

Mr. Mandeville.——Your Lordship greatly mis-
takes my meaning; surely you cannot think I
want to rob my father of any part of his fortune!
in any case I should blush to think of it.——
In the present, any addition to mine, would be
absolutely unnecessary; you do not perhaps guess
my fortune to be so large as it is.

Lord Belmont.——I never heard what it was,
but I suppose you to have thirty or forty Thousand Pounds; as I heard there was a large property lately arrived for your use.

Mr. Mandeville.——I have not the particulars
of

of my fortune about me; I gave them laſt night to my father; when your Lordſhip peruſes them, you will ſee that ſum is but a ſmall part of the wealth Heaven has beſtowed upon me.—I want no addition to it; I would have an ample proviſion made for my dear child; and the reſt, properly ſettled on Miſs Howard and her children.

Lord Belmont.——Emily muſt not be unportioned; it would be ungencrous in me to permit it; however, I will talk this matter over with the Colonel.

They went together to Lady Belmont's dreſſing room.

She confeſſed to me, delighted as ſhe was by their intelligence; ſhe felt the tears ready to flow, on the recollection of that union which had been once ſo near; and was ſo fatally prevented! but like poor Aurelia:

She

She ' facrificed to Heaven's high will,

 ' Each foothing weaknefs of a parent's breaft ;

 ' The figh foft memory prompts: the tender tear,

 ' That ftreaming o'er an óbject lov'd and loft,

 ' With mournful magic, tortures and delights.'


and with a fweet gracioufnefs, which gilds every
act of her's, fhe defired to be herfelf the meffenger to Emily, of tidings fhe believed would give
her pleafure.

The gentlemen walked out to meet Colonel
Mandeville, whom they faw in the park.

The Colonel received my Lord's acquiefcence
to his fon's defire, with unfeigned joy..

Mr. Mandeville left them to fettle preliminaries,
and flew to affure his beloved, his future life
fhould be devoted to her happinefs.

I foon after joined the happy pair ; whom I
found

found indulging their dear little girl; whom Mr. Mandeville was teaching to call Mifs Howard her mama.

I could not help remarking he fighed, when he pronounced the tender appellation; and I hope Emily is too juft, to repine at this proof, that even his attachment to her, cannot wholly obliterate the remembrance of his dear Agnes.

We all met at dinner, with countenances enlightened by joy; even poor Lady Belmont was enlivened, by the unufual cheerfulnefs that exhilarated Mr. Mandeville's fpirits, to an uncommon flow of vivacity.

His converfation is always entertaining:— but then, it was entertainment, unalloyed by one painful idea.

He and Emily walked out with the lovely little child, when fhe had partaken of the defert, and we all joined in praifing him, in whofe charaĉter

the

the fon, the parent, friend and lover, appear in their moft amiable light.

To-morrow we are to be all formality; Lady Mary is a good woman; but her breeding is that of Queen Ann's Court ; and little fuits the *fans ceremonious* manners of,

Dear Sir,

Your obedient humble fervant,

Anne Wilmott.

To

To Mr. HERBERT.

I FORETOLD that Lady Mary's civility would embarrafs us; but I could not forefee her Ladyfhip would have been fo very abfurd as fhe has, begging her pardon, fhewn herfelf; but, thank kind fortune, fhe is gone—fhe ftayed but two days.

She was difgufted to fee the family, what fhe called, infenfible of their late lofs—fhe took every poffible opportunity of reminding them of it.

She behaved with a formal diftant civility to Mr. Mandeville, but feemed to confider him as an ufurper of her darling Harry's place; and, once, pretty plainly hinted, fhe thought there was not fufficient proof of his identity.

He

He had, however, the good fenfe not to feem
to fee- her Ladyfhip's coldnefs to him; and,
by his addrefs and infinuating fweetnefs, without
defcending to fervility, he fo far won her Ladyfhip's good opinion, that fhe vouchfafed to fay,
fhe began to believe he really was Colonel Mandeville's fon; for, he certainly was very like
the Colonel's wife; who, by the way, Lady
Belmont informs me, never was a favorite with
Lady Mary,. though a moft amiable woman.

To me fhe openly avowed the horror fhe felt at
feeing fuch cheerful faces in deep mourning;
—it appeared to her, a flight to the memories of
Lady Julia,. and. her admired Harry.

I affured her Ladyfhip, if fhe would attend
more clofely to the fenfations of her friends,
and not judge by outward appearances, fhe
would fee that every heart ftill felt deeply for
their lofs; though they thought it ungrateful to
Providence, not to receive with gratitude the
blefflng:

bleffings which had been fo mercifully beftowed upon them!

All my rhetoric was loft upon her; and, with real joy, I heard her declare her intention of returning home; however, fhe conquered herfelf fo far, as to wifh Emily and Mr. Mandeville much happinefs; and gave them a civil, though not warm, invitation to Firr Grove.

### IN CONTINUATION.

I have, this day, a letter to inform me, Lord Melvin and my niece are united, and are gone to London—I fhall foon follow—fettlements are drawing for Mr. Mandeville and Emily.

It is determined, that the wedding fhall be private—any pompous buftle would infpire us with melancholy ideas; which, though they might pleafe Lady Mary, would, in my opinion be unfuitable to the occafion.

To-morrow

To-morrow the child is to be baptifed, at my Lord's requeft—it was deferred till his return from the trial.

We are returned from church.

The fweet infant was led into church by her father, in her ufual drefs, only her black orna- ments were exchanged for white ones, of the fame form.

Mr. Mandeville prefented her to Lady Bel- mont, when the ceremony began.

When the clergyman took the poor child, fhe looked frightened, and turned pale.

When Lady Belmont was afked her name, her Ladyfhip, with great fortitude, pronounced, ' Agnes—' Julia—.'

The laft word, to be fure, trembled on her lips, and was fpoken rather lower than the firft.

When

When the dear little angel felt the water, she burſt into tears, and held out her pretty arms to her father, as if to ſave her.

After the ceremony was performed, he took her in his arms, and ſoon huſhed her terrors, by preſſing her to his boſom; and never did I ſee paternal affection look ſo lovely, as in his delighted countenance!

The ſmiles of innocence, and the natural roſes, ſoon returned to the little charmer.

Mr. Ware ſpent the day with us; and re-joiced to hear the little Agnes was ſoon to be bleſſed with a tender mother's care.

After dinner, when Mr. Mandeville, Emily, and the new made Chriſtian were taking their uſual walk, we told Mr. Ware how greatly we had been entertained, and affected, by Mrs. Mandeville's hiſtory.

He

He affured us, that it could give us but a faint idea of her worth—her modefty would not permit her to do herfelf juftice ;—he added,

‘ I arrived at Amfterdam, a few days before
‘ her death.

‘ I found my friend abforbed with grief, as
‘ he plainly faw her fituation.

‘ She requefted fome converfation with me—
‘ her fenfes being quite perfect.

‘ She began, by intreating I would be her
‘ hufband's comforter ; faid, fhe was perfectly
‘ fenfible of her fituation ; that as fhe had been
‘ the happieft of women—the moft beloved of
‘ wives, I muft believe it was painful to be thus
‘ early taken from all her foul held dear ; but,
‘ raifing her voice, fne faid—

‘ I muft die fome time !—that is the fitteft
‘ time, that God appoints !—he will protect my
‘ child,

‘ child, and reward my hufband for all his good-
‘ nefs.’

‘ Take thefe papers, faid fhe; deliver them
‘ to his beft friends ; they will but faintly fpeak
‘ his merits ; but, I truft, there will be feen
‘ fufficient to juftify me, for leaving all that a
‘ woman holds dear, to unite with fuch tender-
‘ nefs, truth and goodnefs, as will be found in
‘ his charaĉter.

‘ I am happy in the belief he will be a tender
‘ father to my dear infant.

‘ I have no fears but for him !—oh ! endea-
‘ vour to mitigate his forrows !—conduĉt him to,
‘ his father, for I truft he has one ftill living ;
‘ and advife my beloved to fupply my place ;—
‘ oh ! may he find a heart that will love him
‘ as fincerely as mine has done !”

‘ Her dejeĉted hufband entering, fhe faid no
‘ more to me, but held out her burning hand to
‘ him.

‘ He

' He pressed it, with sighs, to his heaving
' bosom ; then, with a weak voice, she said—

' Be comforted, my love! listen to your
' friend's advice ; we must submit to the will of
' Heaven.'

' I left them, for a few minutes, to regain
' composure to fulfil my duty to my friend.

' After this, she spoke but seldom ; and the
' next day she grew delirious, and expired the
' following morning.

' I cannot—I wish not to paint Mandeville's
' deep affliction—there was a serenity in his
' grief that shocked me !—sorrow is more alarm-
' ing when it is silent and calm.

' He told me, he purposed to return to
' Youngland.

' I did not think it proper, at first, to seem to
' oppose his own plans ; but hinted, in subse-
                                    ' quent

' quent converfations, that I feared it might ha-
' zard the child's life, to take fuch a voyage,
' and fo long a journey, without a mother's ten-
' der care; befides, I thought he would reflect
' on himfelf, in a calmer hour, for not having
' fought for his father.

' With that candour he fo thoroughly pof-
' feffes, he thanked me, for reminding him of
' his duty, both to his parent, and his child;
' and, indeed, to his departed angel, who had
' ftrongly urged him to purfue his original inten-
' tions.

' He faid, he was afhamed of his pufillanimity
' that made him fhrink from duties fo impor-
' tant---called me his true friend, for teaching
' his wayward will the right path; but I cannot
' leave this place yet, faid he, I cannot fhew my-
' felf to my father, and my friends, in the irra-
' tional ftate of mind I am now in---I had need
' of my moft perfect underftanding to regain
' my father's affection !

' I told

' I told him, I had fo much bufinefs to tranf-
' act with my brother, on his account, as well
' as my own, that I fhould neceffarily be detain-
' ed fome weeks at Amfterdam; when that was
' over, I would leave it to him, to fix the time
' of our removal.

' All the hours I could fpare from this bufinefs,
' I devoted to confoling Mr. Mandeville; fome-
' times I read to him, fometimes I talked to him,
' of the affairs that detained me.

' When he was able to go out,—for his health
' was for fome time greatly injured by the fhock
' he had fuftained, the going to an Englifh
' church, feemed to afford the greateft confola-
' tion.

' As the fondling his child yielded his only
' amufement, by degrees, he became able to
' read; and then applied fo clofely to his books,
' that I feared it would be prejudicial to his
' health and fpirits; however, I had the plea-
' fure

' fure to fee his appetite mend ; and his peace
' of mind in fome degree recover.

' After about two months refidence at Amfter-
' dam, we arrived in London.

' I immediately brought him to Meadow-houfe,
' thinking country air better for his health ;
' and knowing retirement was better fuited to
' his fpirits, than the buftle of the metropolis.

' In the mean time, I made it my bufinefs to
' fearch for his father ; I learned he was living,
' but in heavy affliction for the lofs of his fon ;
' fit time thought I, to comfort him with another
' fon ; but upon mature deliberation, I con-
' fidered it better, to let my friend's fpirits and
' health be more firmly eftablifhed, before I in-
' troduced him to a parent who was finking un-
' der a recent affliction.

' I therefore, the more readily complied with
' his requeft, of getting fome worthy divine, to
' inftruct him in the tenets of religion ; with
                                    ' which

' which he confeſſed himſelf greatly unacquaint-
' ed; though his life had been a ſeries of the
' practice of thoſe virtues, that religion recom-
' mends.

' 'The worthy Mr. Gray, at my requeſt, un-
' dertook this taſk; knowing him by the name
' of Woodville; as my friend had previouſly
' declared his reſolution of never reaſſuming his
' family name, till reſtored to his father's fa-
' vour: and though he had long before, told
' his poor wife, ſhe muſt expect to be called
' Mandeville, whenever ſhe was preſented to
' his family, yet, he had requeſted her to con-
' ceal his real name from every other perſon.

' To me, it was neceſſary it ſhould be known,
' on account of the buſineſs I had undertaken to
' tranſact for him.

' Providence has planned the uhappy meeting
' between Mr. Mandeville and his friends! and
' left me nothing farther to do, than to rejoice
                                                    ' in

‘ in events fo likely to make him as happy, as
‘ he deferves to be.’


We thanked Mr. Ware, for his additional
information ; and (as human nature is apt to go
from one extreme to the other) Lord Belmont
began to condemn his former ideas, of fo much
care being neceffary, to form the perfect character.—faying,


‘ We fee in Mr. Mandeville, to what a height
‘ virtue and accomplifhments can attain ; without
‘ any other help, than a good difpofition, and
‘ a naturally found underftanding.’


‘ Pardon me, my Lord, faid Colonel Belville,
‘ if I do not allow the juftice of your inference.---
‘ One example is not fufficient to demonftrate
‘ fo important a point ; I moft readily grant,
‘ who indeed, can be fo blind as to deny it ?
‘ that Mr. Mandeville has every virtue, and every

N                              ‘ accom-

‘ accomplifhment, which can adorn the beft
‘ educated man! but are we from thence, to
‘ conclude, all men would be polifhed and ami-
‘ able, if left to themfelves.

‘ Mr. Mandeville was born the hero and the
‘ philofopher; and the gentlenefs of his nature
‘ fupplied the want of polifh : but yet, I cannot
‘ give up the neceffity of a good education.

‘ In England, at leaft, I am certain we might
‘ as well expect pine apples on a crab tree, as
‘ good judgment, and proper conduct, from un-
‘ cultivated nature.’

The return of Mandeville and his Emily,
ftopped our farther difcourfe upon the fubject.

We converfed the reft of the day, with that
cheerfulnefs, which cafe, love and fri ndfhip,
can alone create! feldom enjoyed, and never
well defcribed, as relaters and readers have
                                    different

different tastes and different feelings, which it is vain to attempt to gratify; yet, such society, when accompanied with a harmony of disposition, which enclines each person to endeavour to please, gives me the clearest idea I can form, of the conversation of ' just men made perfect :' and must, I think, resemble it the most any earthly enjoyment can; because, it can be experienced only by ' the pure in heart.'

Expect no more letters from me; Colonel Belville's lawyer informs him, that every thing is ready for figning and fealing the important deeds: and as the writings for the marriage of Mr. Mandeville and Miss Howard, cannot be completed in less than a month, my gentleman insists upon my going from hence directly; so either to please him, or myself, I shall begin to practice obedience now, that it may sit the easier upon me hereafter; and therefore I have consented to go to London, on Monday; and the rather, as Lady Sarah Mordaunt is unhappy at

the

the thoughts of the marriage being celebrated
here.'

A little fuperftition will, fometimes, inhabit
the breaft of an old woman!

She has conceived ftrange terrors from the
paft fhocking fcenes ; and her exceffive fondnefs
for the nephew (to whom fhe has always fupplied
the place of a mother) gives her a fort of right,
to have even her whims indulged.

I confefs, I had fet my heart on Lord Belmont's giving my hand, to the man who has fo
long poffeffed my heart ; but fo he takes it from
fomebody, I will be content.

I fhall not leave Belmont without regret ; but
after the long experience I have had of Belville's
affection ; and the confcioufnefs, that he has
fubmitted to my will and pleafure, with very uncommon patience, it would be difingenuous not

to

to own, I have no wiſh to poſtpone an event, from which I expeＣt an increaſe of happineſs to, .

Your's, &c.

ANNE WILMOTT.

To Mrs. MANDEVILLE.

I HOPE you, and Lady Belmont, received my congratulations, and thofe of my beloved, to Lord Belmont, and Mr. Mandeville, two pofts ago:——they were very fincere, though very concife.

You cannot need any flowers of rhetoric, to convince you, we fhared in your happinefs; but you, who by marrying privately, and in the country, have efcaped the hurry, confufion, and turbulence of joy I have lived in, for this laft month, will, perhaps, not fo eafily credit how little time the buftle of congratulations has left me to write at all; much lefs tcwrite floridly

and

and copioufly, even on a fubject which interefted me fo much as your nuptials.

However, as all things muft have an end, the joy which has been expreffed by our mutual friends, has fubfided fufficiently, to give me leave to take up my pen with more compofure.

Lady Melvin and I are almoft conftantly together.

She is happy in the polite attentions of her Lord; and, I really believe, poffeffes his fincere affection, as he certainly does her's.

She accompanies me in a round of vifits of ceremony :---in fome of thofe, I have been highly entertained at your's, and your beloved honorable's expence.

Do not look grave, my dear Emily, but enjoy, as I have done, the ridiculous comments on your match.

I have

I have been affured by fome, who protefted they had the account from the beft authority, ‘ that Mifs Howard, a niece of Lady Belmont's, ‘ a beautiful young creature, but juft fifteen, ‘ was, laft week, barbaroufly facrificed, againft ‘ her will, to an old man turned of feventy !--- ‘ an odious Indian too!

‘ He pretended, indeed, to be of the Mande- ‘ ville family, and heir at law to Lord Belmont's ‘ eftate, and title ; but it was well known, his ‘ birth was fpurious ; and, as to his riches, it ‘ was believed, they would prove counterfeit ‘ alfo ; for it was an undoubted fact, that a weal- ‘ thy merchant fupported him, and had lent ‘ him large fums, to obtain the prize of Mifs ‘ Howard's hand, which would enfure him Lord ‘ Belmont's fortune.

‘ Poor girl ! they fay fhe fhines in jewels ; ‘ alas ! how will the unfortunate victim be mor- ‘ tified, when, like the jay in the fable fhe is ftrip- ‘ ped of her borrowed plumes !

‘ It

' It is wonderful, how a man of Lord Bel-
' mont's good underſtanding, allowed penetra-
' tion, and knowledge of the world, can have
' been ſo impoſed upon.'

I was malicious enough to liſten in ſilence to
this curious tale.

The conſequence has been, that Lord Melvin
was informed, the next day, that I was quoted
for it's author !

I long to have you appear in the drawing-
room, in all your Eaſtern magnificence, with
your handſome, and youthful huſband ; that I
may ſee whether theſe wonderfully well-informed
goſſips can bluſh at their own effrontery !

Come up ſoon, I entreat you ; if not for this
purpoſe, come to give the only addition that is
wanting to the happineſs of

   Your truly affectionate,

     ANNE BELVILLE.

        To

To Mrs. S——.

I HAVE now, my dear madam, finished the task of transcribing the papers I received from Lady Anne Belville.

I ought, indeed, to call it by another name; as, I must confess, exclusive of the pleasure the endeavouring to oblige you must always give me, I have found much satisfaction in writing accounts of events and characters so interesting as these have proved.

I have taken the liberty of leaving out many of Emily's epistles to her friend, Miss Kitty Fortescue, as they were chiefly repetitions of what was recited in Lady Anne's letters to Mr. Herbert.

Lady

Lady Anne has fulfilled her promise of adding some particulars, which could not be found in these manuscripts, and, as I am convinced you must be thoroughly interested in all that relates to this worthy family, I will transmit them to you in her own words.

‘ Lord and Lady Belmont reside entirely in
‘ the country; and as the house of Belmont is
‘ sufficiently large to admit of it, have persuaded
‘ Mr. and Mrs. Mandeville to spend most of
‘ their time with them.

‘ They have, however, an elegant small
‘ lodge on Mr. Mandeville’s estate, to which
‘ they sometimes retire for a month at a time—
‘ longer, they think it unkind to leave Belmont,
‘ as they are sensible, they alone can keep the
‘ spirits of that amiable pair from sinking ; and,
‘ as Mrs. Mandeville promised her beloved Lady
‘ Julia, not to forsake her parents, she would
‘ herself be unhappy in a long absence.

‘ Colonel

' Colonel Mandeville's fpirits were, at firft,
' roufed by the return of his fon fo unexpected-
' ly; but they have funk again!

' He has not that ftrong affiftance which true
' religion gives, and which has enabled Lord
' and Lady Belmont to conquer their afflic-
' tion!

' Colonel Mandeville is a ftrict moralift; but
' revelation has not had its proper influence on
' his mind! and morality, alone, is not fuffici-
' ent to teach patience in adverfity; and to in-
' fpire that comfort which arifes from a pious
' truft in God!

' To this caufe I afcribe the return of his
' dejection;—the world have affigned another
' reafon, viz.

' That, though Mr. Mandeville is the very
' beft of fons, and continues the moft exalted of
' characters, yet, that the Colonel feels himfelf
' mortified, at feeing his darling Harry excelled
' by

' by a young man, who had never been a favo-
' rite, and who had never received the benefit
' of his inftructions.'

'This fentiment would fhew a littlenefs of
' mind, that I verily believe him incapable of;
' but yet, I fear, his poor Harry's beloved form
' ftill haunts his imagination; and will not per-
' mit him to reap all the happinefs he might now
' enjoy!

'Emily is as happy a wife as myfelf, which is
' faying all I know how to defcribe.

'Her own two lovely boys are not dearer to
' her, than the charming Agnes; who is, with-
' out exception, the moft delightful creature I
' ever beheld!.

'Her form is fo perfect, that fhe might be
' chofen as a model for a ftatuary to copy.

'Her face is not fo beautiful from its fine
' features, faultlefs as thefe are, as it is from

' expref-

' expreſſion---it is the index of a lively and en-
' gaging mind.

' Her underſtanding, and diſpoſition, pro-
' miſe that the fruit will be equal to the bloſ-
' ſom!

' The family at Belmont are ſo happy in
' themſelves, and the ſociety of Mr. Ware,
' Mr. Herbert, and Mr. Gray, that they do
' not extend their acquaintance farther than
' civility requires.

' Lady Mary Mandeville has paid that debt
' to nature, which all are ſome day to pay.

' She left her large fortune to Lord Belmont.

' She never was cordially attached to any
' body but her brother, and her admired Harry.

' Colonel Belville and myſelf, are annual viſi-
' tors at Belmont; and, as I cannot go without

' my

' my four little prattlers, we make a large party---
' but it is a happy one.

   ' Conjugal love, and parental affection, with
' all the joys which friendship, founded upon
' virtue, can yield, prevents our ever feeling
' that fashionable disease, called *ennui*; which,
' epidemical as it plainly is, amongst our great
' people, finds no cure in a round of diffipation
' and amusements, as they call their avocations;
' and, I fear, they are not, in general, quali-
' fied to try our never-failing recipé.'

   I will now, my dear Mrs. S——, lay down
my pen, and sincerely wish you may receive
from it, the pleasure this long use of it has
given to

      Your sincerely affectionate

               JANE P——.

    F I N I S.

www.ingramcontent.com/pod-product-compliance
Lightning Source LLC
Chambersburg PA
CBHW021047030726
47496CB00006B/1724